HATTIE + OLAF

Frida Nilsson • Illustrated by Stina Wirsén

HATTIE + OLAF

Translated by Julia Marshall

GECKO PRESS

Horse fever

There's a pear tree in the schoolyard in Hardemo. Actually, there are several, but this particular tree is the tallest and has a fork at the top. It's perfect for two people to sit in. There isn't room for a third.

Hattie and Linda sit in the fork almost every break time. They grab small, tart pears from the branches and throw the cores so they rattle down through the lilac bushes.

Hattie and Linda are best friends. They have been since the first day of school, and now they're already in their second year.

In one way they're alike. Neither of them knows when to keep quiet. But they're not alike at all to look at. Hattie has straight, brown hair. Her ears stick out like two big coins and her nose is as round as a potato.

Linda is small. Her hair is blonde and messy. Her teeth are as big as sugar cubes and she has a turned-up nose that twitches. Her mother stays at home all day sewing sleeve holders for a factory—they're elastic bands to hold your sleeves out of the way. When Linda comes home her mother is very tired. She can hardly even talk or play.

"I wish my mother was more like yours," says Linda, biting into her pear.

Hattie's mother sleeps all day. But she wakes up when Hattie comes home from school and she has enough energy for most things. She needs a lot of sleep because she works nights at the hospital in town. She sees the most terrible things. Once she saw a man who fell asleep while he was squatting. He slept for two days and his legs turned blue. And then they had to cut off his legs!

Hattie shudders to think of it. She doesn't ever want to work at the hospital. But her mother is tougher than most. That's because she grew up with three big brothers who she had to fight with every day. The brothers, called Nisse, Janne and Olle, are grown-ups now. And they don't fight anymore.

"Mmm..." says Hattie. "What about your father? You have him."

"Oh, he's mostly in the garage," Linda answers, "and only comes in for dinner."

"Roy then?" says Hattie. "You have him."

Roy is Linda's small ugly guinea pig. He lives in a cage.

"That old wreck!" Linda laughs. "He just screams when you try to pat him. I think he's wrong in the head."

Hattie is quiet for a bit. She grabs a pear and sinks her teeth into it. "But you have me. I'm not wrong in the head!"

"Nothing too serious," says Linda, twitching her nose.

Then they laugh till they almost fall out of the fork. A magpie flies squalling from the tree.

There's a sudden rustle in the lower branches. Karin and Ellen stick their heads up.

"We're sitting here by ourselves," says Linda.

Ellen is out of breath. "We're playing horses, do you want to join in?"

Linda twitches her nose. "Nah."

But Hattie tosses away the rest of her pear and starts climbing down. "Might as well."

Linda sighs and climbs down after her.

Something has happened to Hattie this term; well, to almost all the girls in the class. They don't want to do the same things as before. They don't want to play clapping games or football or skipping or tag. All they want to do is run at full gallop around the schoolyard. They snort and toss their heads, rear and kick their hind legs. Their pockets are full of bookmarks with happy horses on them and in their bags are magazines called *Pony*.

They have horse fever.

You can't see it on their body when someone has horse fever. They don't get green boils or a ponytail and four hooves. Horse fever happens in their brain, and it means horses are all they can think about.

Linda is the only one who hasn't got horse fever. She sits on the bench beside the gravel area, kicking her feet while the others play. She wouldn't want a horse if they threw one at her. She'd much rather have a moped, but she's too young. Ellen says girls shouldn't have mopeds. But Linda doesn't care one bit about that.

Ellen, who has glasses, is the happiest in the whole class. She lives in a house called Peaceful Haven and her father is a policeman. But that's not why she's so happy. In the field a little way away from Peaceful Haven is a pony and it belongs to Ellen. The pony is as round as a barrel. It's called Crumb.

Karin has been heaps of times to Peaceful Haven to meet Crumb. That's because Karin and Ellen are best friends.

Now Ellen pulls a stick from the ground. "I'm the trainer!

"I'm Crumb!" says Karin.

"Can't I be Crumb?" says Hattie. "You were yesterday."

"No," says Ellen. "Crumb's my horse; I decide who'll be her."

Hattie sighs.

"You'll have to think up another name," says Karin.

"I can't think of anything," mumbles Hattie.

"You could be Agneta Johansson!" calls Linda. "I know a horse called that!"

Ellen frowns. "You don't," she says.

"Yes, I do!" calls Linda happily.

"Where is this horse, then?" asks Karin.

"Where I live, in Berga! Except both my parents seem to think she's a person, because she looks normal in the daytime. But I was suspicious, and one night I sneaked up on her to check. At midnight she got up in her nightie and opened the fridge. And inside was just hay and carrots! She ate a whole pile, and then she went out and neighed at the moon."

"That's not true!" says Karin.

"Yes, it is," says Linda, happier still. She jumps down. "And do you know how she turned into one? She was *bitten* by a horse when she was small."

Ellen swallows.

"Ha ha!" says Linda. "You've heard of vampires, but you didn't know there's such a thing as horse vampires. Better watch out for that Crumb-ball!"

"She's called Crumb!" shrieks Ellen.

Hattie laughs so hard she shakes.

Ellen hisses and kicks the gravel. "Are you playing or not?"

"Yes," mumbles Hattie.

"Then you can be called Trotter. Now we'll start. Gallop!"

Ellen begins to wave her stick, and Karin and Hattie run around and around, tossing their heads.

"Ne-e-e-e-eigh!" neighs Karin.

"Very good, Crumb," says Ellen. "You're my best horse."

"Can I come and meet Crumb one day?" puffs Hattie.

"Maybe, we'll see," says Ellen.

"Please?"

"We're playing! Horses don't talk! Trot!"

Hattie and Karin slow down to a trot.

Linda sighs and climbs back up the pear tree. She grabs pears without tasting them and throws them instead at the school wall. Sloppy marks appear on the bricks. She hates that stupid horse fever.

Crazy racers, blowflies and riding-school kids

What Hattie wants more than anything is a horse. There are plenty of animals where she lives. Pigs and ducks, hens and sheep, and also the black dog Tacka and the cats, of course. But if only there could be a horse! Life would be much more fun.

But there isn't one. However, there are lots of horses over at the riding school in Riseberga. In Riseberga there used to be a monastery, where nuns walked around with their heads bowed, thinking about God. Now there are only ruins of the monastery. Horses run around with their tails high, thinking about sugar lumps. They might sometimes think about God as well, you never know.

"I'm going to bike to the riding school!" says Hattie one Saturday in August. She puts on her clogs and swings the door open. Outside it smells of tired, old summer. The sun burns down and makes all the walls creak. The stable walls, the henhouse walls, the doghouse walls, the woodshed walls, the hayloft walls and the walls of the house where Hattie lives with her mother and father. Their big red house is called Ängatorp, which means meadow house.

"Ride carefully!" her father calls from the upstairs room. He's working on an article that has to be ready soon for the newspaper.

"Ye-es!" answers Hattie.

Then she gets her bike from the shed. It's called LBC and has one red handle and one green. The strange thing is that LBC stands for Ladies' Bosom Cream. That's what Hattie's cousin Tony says anyway. He's fifteen years old and lives in Hackvad.

Hattie hops on the bike and off she goes. But she doesn't bike carefully! She takes off like a rally driver; dust billows up and stones fly. The forest looms tall and dark along the edge of the ditch.

After a while she turns off Ängatorp's gravel road. Now she has to cross the main road, where trucks sometimes thunder past and teenagers race their cars back and forth making rubber streaks on the asphalt.

She looks quickly in both directions, then darts to the other side.

That goes fine, with no crazy racers in sight. The racers are unpredictable. Once Hattie was watching when they stuck their rear ends out the window. She hates that sort of thing. Tony in Hackvad is obsessed with racing cars. But he doesn't have a car yet, only a moped with brown mudguards. And sometimes he squeezes her hand so hard her fingers crack. He does it to be stupid. Once he even called his mother Britt Birdbutt. You just don't do that.

Now it's all downhill. Her hair flies out behind, the wind pulls at her clothes. The wheels turn faster, faster, faster; she's never biked this fast before! Another road suddenly crosses hers—BANG!

Before she knows it, she's on the ground. Her body is shaking. Her heart is beating like a drum. Her palms sting from the little stones pressed into them. Her knees burn and she's bleeding. The bike wheels are still spinning.

"Ow!" someone groans. There's another bike on

the road. It's a bigger bike and beneath it is a woman wearing boots. Her trousers are torn. She waves her arms, but she doesn't get up.

Hattie gets straight to her feet. She's been stupid, she knows that much. You can't go that fast downhill without looking out for what's ahead.

"You should say sorry," says the woman on the ground. She moans and tries to push her bike away.

Hattie swallows. There's something strange about that word. Other words leap from your mouth as easy as anything. But that word sorry, it sort of gets stuck on the tongue and doesn't want to come out. Especially when someone lying on the ground with torn trousers thinks you *should* say sorry. Then it doesn't come at all.

A tear runs down the woman's cheek. "Help me up!" she cries.

It's as if there's a cold hand squeezing Hattie's heart. She doesn't want to. Adults should help children up, not the other way round. She picks up her bike and pedals quickly away, without saying anything.

"Stop!" shrieks the woman, but Hattie doesn't. She pedals as hard as she can and soon she's around the corner. The woman's cries become fainter.

Tears well up in Hattie. What if the woman dies? What if they find her two weeks from now all white and stiff under her bike. And it's Hattie who killed her. And she didn't even say sorry.

In Riseberga she parks her bike against the stable. It smells strongly of horse dung and sweat. She follows the path over to the ruins. Far ahead she sees brown backs gleaming in the sun. Black tails twitch away flies and there's neighing in the distance.

The nuns who used to walk here never neighed; they'd sworn a vow of silence. They weren't allowed to talk to anyone, only whisper a little to God.

Hattie blinks at the sky. Maybe she could whisper something to God? It wouldn't hurt.

First, she looks all around, to make sure that no one anywhere is listening.

"Dear good God, please make it so that the person I biked into doesn't die. If you do that, I'll never bike off without saying sorry again. I solemnly declare."

At once she feels better. Her heart feels warmer and her legs a little more springy. She tears up some grass and goes over to the gate. A horse trots carefully over. He sniffs the air and then takes the little pile of grass. His muzzle is soft, softer than velvet. His eyes are the brown of chestnuts and his long teeth are like bamboo shoots. He's so beautiful it hurts.

"Don't you think I should start at the riding school?" Hattie asks. "Wouldn't that be fun?"

The horse doesn't say yes. But he doesn't say no either. He nudges her hand for more grass.

But Hattie turns and walks away. She wants to ask the riding instructor if there are any spare places.

The stable is dark and the floor dirty. The stalls are empty, with just a little straw in the corners. The saddle room is as quiet as the grave. There's no sign of any riders.

Hattie goes back out into the light. She looks behind the stable, but there's only a pile of dung. Seven blowflies have gathered for a family party. There will be dung for first course, second course and dessert. Their backs shine like green shields and their tongues are like little straws. Straws for sucking up poo. Hattie hurries away. She likes blowflies as much as she likes crazy racers.

A group of children stand at a fence with black

knobs on their heads. They're wearing boots with high heels. They're the riding-school kids. Happy, well-groomed riding-school kids. They see Hattie standing there in her clogs with no knob on her head. Actually, Hattie doesn't know what she hates most. Crazy racers, blowflies or riding-school kids. But if she could only be one of them, that'd be a different story!

"Do you know where the riding instructor is?" she calls.

The children shake their heads. "She's late today," says a girl with skinny legs. "The lesson should have started a quarter of an hour ago."

So Hattie stands a little way off and waits. She takes no notice of the children staring; she looks the other way.

They must have stood there for an eternity, five minutes or ten, when the girl with the skinny legs reaches and points. "There she is!"

A woman with holes in her trousers is walking up the road. Her hair is ruffled. The bike she's pushing goes *gnii-gnii-gnii*. One wheel is buckled. Hattie stares. It's the woman she ran over! She didn't die!

She stands frozen to the spot as the woman comes closer. The woman narrows her eyes.

"You!" she says. "That's not what you do! When you crash into someone you say sorry!"

Hattie is silent. She can hear God above her whispering, *Psst, don't forget your promise!*

"Well?" the woman hisses. "Do I hear it now?"

"S-s… I wanted to ask if I can come to riding school."

"What did you say?" shrieks the woman.

"I wanted to ask if I could come to riding school," Hattie whispers again.

The woman puts her hands on her hips. "Do you actually think you can start riding school without even saying sorry?!"

The children at the fence stare so hard their eyes are almost popping out of their heads.

But Hattie runs off and leaps onto her bike. As she pedals away there's a great big hole in her stomach. At the bottom of the hole, a word is rattling. It will never come out.

The road is blurry through her tears. To stand and listen to someone shrieking at you to say sorry is the worst thing. With everyone else listening as well! Hattie crosses the big road without meeting any racers this time either. And when she gets home her cheeks are streaked with tears.

Her mother and father are sitting in the kitchen cleaning chanterelle mushrooms.

"What on earth happened?" cries her mother when she sees the dark blood on Hattie's knees. "Did you fall off?"

Hattie tells them everything, snot running from her nose. About crashing into the woman and the children and the sorry that never came. And that the woman yelled that she couldn't go to riding school.

When they've finished listening, her father says that, if you look at it one way, Hattie biked into the woman. But if you look at it the other way, the woman biked into Hattie, and she didn't say sorry either! "No shortage of stupid women," he mutters, letting a bush spider out through the window.

"Yes, and no shortage of stupid men either," says her mother, for balance. Then she stands at the stove and fries mushrooms with salt. They eat the chanterelles from saucers using teeny, tiny forks with only three prongs. And then it starts to rain outside the window. The drops grow bigger and bigger until they're bashing at the panes. Hattie kicks her heels against the sofa. She doesn't know what she likes best. Rain or chanterelles or her mother and father. Maybe she likes them all equally.

Over at the riding school, there are nine soaked children riding their horses round and round in the muck. Their fingers are blue and their teeth chatter.

A woman stands in the middle, with tattered trousers, yelling through the raindrops. And she's thinking how much she hates rain. The worst thing is that the bike waiting for her against the stable wall is broken. She'll have to push it the whole way home in a downpour.

A longhorn wish

The last bit of scab falls off Hattie's knee sometime in September. That's how it is with scabs: they fall off sooner or later, and shouting riding instructors fade from memory if you give them a little time.

But horse fever doesn't go away. At nighttime, Hattie lies sweating and dreaming. "A horse," she mumbles. "My own horse."

During the day she follows her father like a tail, in the field, in the hayloft and among all the dusty books in his office.

"Can we buy a horse?" she asks, tugging his trouser leg.

Poor Papa. Horses are expensive. The cheapest sort costs several thousand. Oh, if he could only find some buried treasure behind the woodshed, or if suddenly it would say on the news: *And horse prices today have dropped by ninety-five percent.*

But no, life is as usual and the wallet in the drawer remains slim.

One day the telephone rings. Hattie answers. "Hello?"

"Hello there, it's Karl-Erik."

Karl-Erik is an old man who lives nearby. He has a red dog called Ronja and twenty white geese that honk around the yard. He's nice. But inside the cabin it's almost black with dirt. He doesn't have a real bathroom either; you have to go outside.

Karl-Erik wants to talk to her father.

Hattie runs out to the woodshed. Splinters fly and logs somersault when her father's axe hits them. There's a lot of wood to be chopped before winter.

"Telephone," says Hattie.

Papa wipes the sweat from his brow and stamps off.

"Can we buy a horse?" calls Hattie.

Papa just shakes his head. He doesn't know what to say anymore.

Hattie stays sitting in the woodshed, looking at

the stack of wood. A small creature with long antennae clambers onto one of the logs. A longhorn. It's a beetle so rare that you almost never see them. Hattie puts it on her finger. The beetle looks at her for a moment. It poops on her finger and flies up to the wood stack. It disappears among the logs.

When a ladybug flies from your finger you can wish for something, Hattie thinks. But a beetle like this is much rarer than a ladybug. So it must be even better to wish on a longhorn beetle.

She closes her eyes. Papa can finally afford a horse. Her own horse with a smooth coat and glossy mane. That's what she wishes for.

The beetle up in the wood stack waves its antennae. They swivel this way and that. Then it dies, because that's what longhorn beetles do in autumn.

The woodshed door flies open! Her father has pink cheeks and shining eyes. "Come on," he says. "Hop in the car."

Hattie follows him, curious. "What are we doing?"

"Going to Karl-Erik's," Papa says.

"What will we do there?"

"I need to borrow a trailer."

"What for?"

Papa smiles. "You'll see."

The whole way to Karl-Erik's, her father smiles that way. He whistles and drums his fingers on the steering wheel.

"Let's see now," he says.

When they swing into the yard, the geese run away with their tails wagging. They hiss and poke their tongues out at the blue car. But Ronja bounds over like a red blizzard.

Karl-Erik doesn't bound at all. "Ow-ow-ow," he mutters as he limps through the mud. He has a leg that gets stiff sometimes. It's been like that since he was young and got an iron rod stuck in his leg. It went right through and came out the other side. His leg looked like a sausage on a stick!

Karl-Erik has a pointed beard and big ears.

"She's behind the outhouse," he says. "But I can't

drag her out myself, she's a real monster."

When he says she, he means the trailer. That's how he talks.

Papa strides away and comes back shortly with the stock trailer. He clamps it onto the car's tow bar. "I'll be off then," he says. "Hattie, please be kind and help Karl-Erik while I'm gone. It's hard for him with his leg."

Hattie nods. Of course she'll be kind. That's not hard!

When the car disappears, they go inside the cabin. The lamp in the window glows feebly through its greasy glass shade. The bench is covered in muck. There's a bucket on the floor with a fish skeleton and crusts of bread in it. Flies crowd around the warm oven.

Karl-Erik takes his floppy little purse from the kitchen drawer. "Listen, would you go to the shop and buy potatoes for me? You'd be an angel."

Angel. It's not often Hattie gets called that kind of thing. Hearing the word, she can almost feel wings growing on her back. She nods and takes the money from Karl-Erik. "Of course," she says.

"Buy ten," says Karl-Erik. "And mind you don't get run over."

When Hattie goes out on the road, she keeps her back straight and smiles a little so it only just shows. And everyone who goes past probably thinks, There goes a real angel.

It's quite a way to Åbytorp and the farm shop. When she finally arrives the sun is low on the horizon. A bell jingles in the doorway.

The farm shop is a lovely place; it has everything you could wish for. Cakes and soap and nails and sandpaper. Tins of soup and crayons. Hattie goes back and forth between the shelves. She runs her hand over all the things and breathes in the smells.

Suddenly something rustles under her hand. Bags of gumdrops. The sour kind.

Her mouth waters. And that rustling, which is the gumdrops' own language, she knows what it means: *Buy me! Buy me!*

She picks up the bag. *I only cost four-fifty!* it rustles. You know how good it is when bright, sour fruits get stuck between your teeth and make your mouth pucker up with sugar?

Hattie runs for a basket. She can't help it; the rustling bag has made her forget that she should only be buying potatoes.

With the gumdrops in the basket, she carries on. Soon she sees a big box of potatoes on the floor. "One, two, three, four, five, six, seven, eight, nine, ten." She knots the plastic bag and heads for the counter.

Just then something stops her, something lying in pink, perfect rows. It also says: *Buy me! Buy me! I taste like strawberries. You can chew me forever or blow a bubble, a bubble that bursts over your nose and gets stuck in your hair! Won't that be fun!*

Hattie swallows. Of course, it would be great to have a pack of bubble gum as well. But she already has the gumdrops.

So what? says the bubble gum. *I only cost two-fifty! Do you understand how little money that is?*

With a shaking hand, Hattie takes a pack and puts it in her basket. She can't help it, she has to.

The man at the counter stares at the things. His nose is full of black dots. He counts everything up and says, "That will be twelve."

Hattie holds up her note. "I only have ten."

The man's eyes drill into her. "Then you'll have to put something back."

Hattie looks at the three things with a sorrowful heart. Which one should she put back?

Not me, say the gumdrops. *You have to keep me!*

The bubble gum says the same thing. *You can't put me back when I taste so good!*

The potatoes lie in a heap and sigh. *Who cares about me?* they say. Potatoes are probably the most boring thing there is.

"The potatoes," says Hattie in a dry voice.

The man puts away the potatoes, counts again and says, "Seven."

Hattie takes the change and hurries out. Straightaway, she opens the bag and puts a sour fruit in her mouth. It's green and tastes heavenly. But as she plods along the road, she can feel tears coming. It was wrong to put the potatoes back, she knows that. And Karl-Erik gave her his last ten. The sour fruits don't taste sweet now, they taste salty because so many tears are running down her cheeks and into her mouth. Dread gnaws inside her. What will happen when Karl-Erik sees what she's done?

No, she can't even think about it. She dare not ever go back to the cabin. She sits in a damp ditch and howls.

It's not long before her body starts to shake with cold. The sun has gone down, and her toes are numb. People who go past don't think, That's an angel sitting there. They think, There sits an ugly child stuffing herself with sugar until her teeth turn black. She's been sitting on the bubble gum, so it's gone flat. It's getting dark in the bushes.

Suddenly someone is calling:

"Hattie!"

It's Karl-Erik.

"Hattie!"

"Ye-es!" shouts Hattie.

First Ronja comes running. A moment later Karl-Erik catches up. He has a crutch under one arm. "Why are you sitting here?" he asks.

Hattie can't answer, she just cries. Then Karl-Erik sees the bag Ronja is chewing on.

"Oh, I see," he says. "I understand. Had they run out of potatoes at the shop?"

"Yes, something like that," Hattie whispers, and hands him the coins.

Karl-Erik helps her out of the ditch. They limp slowly back to the house, poor old Karl-Erik and Hattie, the angel who should have bought potatoes. Ronja runs ahead with her tail in the air.

Then they sit on the bench outside Karl-Erik's cabin, chewing bubble gum.

Suddenly there's tooting on the road. Papa's back!

He swings into the yard with the stock trailer behind him. It shakes and rattles, and something slams into the wall. *Bang!* Hattie leaps up. "What have you got in there?" she asks.

Her father smiles. "Have you had a good time while I've been away?" he asks. "Has Hattie been kind?"

Karl-Erik nods. "She has," he says. "Hattie went all the way to the shop to buy some things for me."

"Really, that's nice," says her father.

"Mm," says Karl Erik. "I happened to have run out of bubble gum."

Then Papa looks confused, but luckily there's another *bang* in the trailer, so he forgets to ask anymore about it.

Then Hattie hears a sound...hooves, stamping nervously on the trailer floor.

"A horse?" whispers Hattie.

Papa starts whistling and Karl-Erik giggles. He knows what's inside the trailer; you can tell.

Things start swirling in Hattie's head. Did Papa go and get a horse? Did he finally get enough money? She climbs into the back seat of the car with jelly legs. When the car rolls away, she forgets to wave to Karl-Erik. All she can think about is the thing in the trailer, kicking.

Papa drives carefully. He keeps looking in the rearview mirror.

A horse, a horse, a horse. Her heart goes at a trot and a canter; never has a car journey taken so long. When at last they roll into Ängatorp's gravel road, she jumps up and down in the back seat and shrieks: "A horse, a horse! At last!"

Papa backs through the gate into the field. "Hold yourself together," he says.

He opens the latch … Something kicks anxiously with its hooves … Papa puts his hand on the door … He opens it …

Nothing comes out. Hattie waits a few moments. Then she creeps up and peeps in.

There's a bony creature inside. With ears as long as a rabbit's. At the end of its tail is a shaggy tassel. Its mane is short and stubby. The brown, almond-shaped eyes look at her for a moment.

Hattie's mouth falls open. It's not a horse.

The thing that's not a horse raps its hooves a couple of times, lets out an angry squeal and bares its teeth.

"Heeee-haaaaw!"

It crashes out of the trailer. Hattie watches it buck around the field.

"A donkey?" she says.

Her father nods proudly.

A donkey, yes. That's what you get when you wish on a tired old longhorn beetle instead of a ladybug. And now the donkey has moved in to Ängatorp, although he doesn't look at all pleased about it. The sheep run in terror from this ugly thing, which appears to be a monster. The donkey clacks its teeth and races after them. And what is the donkey called? Yes, his name is Olaf.

The story of Olaf

It was Karl-Erik who told Papa on the phone about Olaf. Olaf lived with a nasty man called Persson. He was as stingy as a snake and didn't give Olaf nearly enough oats. One day Persson had to empty the outhouse bucket. As he went through the garden the bottom fell out of the bucket, so all the poop went onto his shoes. At that exact moment, Olaf squealed, which sounded like laughing, so Persson went over and kicked Olaf. Since then, Olaf has been furious. Papa rang Persson and asked how much Olaf would cost. Only five hundred.

"Poor old thing. He hasn't had an easy time," says Papa when he and Hattie go out with the bucket of oats. It's Monday and the sun has hardly risen above the stable roof. "But if you're good with animals, you can tame anything. And besides, you almost have a horse now!"

Almost a horse? No, this much Hattie knows: she doesn't almost have a horse! A horse can only be a horse! A horse has a beautiful, smooth coat and a long, shiny tail. You love a horse and a horse always loves you back.

But a donkey is just a wreck! Donkeys have fur on their backs and stupid buck teeth. Who, by the way, has ever heard of donkey magazines, or donkey bookmarks that you swap with your friends? Hattie is shaking with rage and her eyes are so tired they hurt because on top of everything Olaf spent all night bellowing like an idiot. No one could sleep. Hattie wants to throw the bucket of oats in the ditch and say that she doesn't want an almost-horse! But Papa looks so pink and pleased. His eyes are shining. He's proud of course, and he'd never have enough money for a horse.

There's no sign of the sheep in the field. They were shocked when Olaf arrived. Now they're probably lying over in the clump of trees. Olaf stands beside the gate, switching his tail.

"Heeee-haawwww!"

Papa gives Hattie a crust. "Let's see if you can make friends with him now."

Hattie wrinkles her nose. "I don't want to."

"Come on, he's as scared of you as you are of him," says Papa.

Hattie sighs. She sticks the crust under Olaf's muzzle. Olaf snorts. He decides to gnaw on the gate instead. He's so stupid he doesn't care if he gets splinters in his mouth.

"Try to be nice now," says Hattie.

Nice? Olaf isn't nice—he's furious! He squeals and starts running around in circles. The grass quivers and a crow in the top of a birch tree flies up in terror.

She turns to her father. "It's no good. He's crazy."

Papa laughs. He shakes the bucket of oats and steps in through the gate. Olaf tosses his head like a bull.

"Careful," squeaks Hattie.

"There, there, there you go." Papa's voice is calm and deep. He steps carefully closer to Olaf.

Suddenly Hattie sees that Papa is right. Olaf really is afraid! He backs away. His mouth quivers, and his eyes blink meekly.

"I'm not going to treat you badly," says Papa, following him. In the end they go quite a long way into the field. Olaf stops at last. "Look!" calls Papa. "He's starting to calm down. You can see what being good with animals looks like!"

Then Olaf bares his teeth and bellows!

"Heeeee-hawwww!"

And now Hattie hears what that nasty Persson heard. It's a laugh! He's laughing at them, at Papa, who thought Olaf would be afraid of little old him. He rears and sets off at a gallop.

Papa throws away the bucket and the oats fly, and then he runs for his life!

"Hurry! Before you die!" shrieks Hattie.

Olaf rushes after him, clacking his jaw.

At the last second Papa leaps over the gate. He lands with a thud on the grass. Olaf crashes headfirst into the fence.

He shakes himself and staggers off.

"Are you all right?" asks Hattie.

Her father slowly gets to his feet. "Heck, what a beast," he puffs. "He's more impossible than I thought. But patience is the thing. And the school bus will be here any minute."

They hurry back through the wilted garden. The sunflowers are brown shafts standing in the beds. When they reach the road, the bus is rumbling around the corner.

"I'll bet you can't wait to tell your class about Olaf," Papa says.

Hattie turns cold. She's thought she won't mention Olaf. She can just imagine what they'll say if they hear that a donkey has moved into Ängatorp. Ellen and Karin will probably laugh themselves sick. No one else in Hardemo has a donkey.

She looks at her father. His hair is sticking up after the dance with Olaf. His trousers have grass stains. But he's still smiling and standing proud and tall. He'd be so sad he'd crumple up if he knew that Hattie was ashamed of being given a donkey.

"Sure," she mumbles.

The bus stops with a hiss in front of the house. Hattie climbs on and her father waves through the window. "See you this afternoon!" he calls. "Then you can tell me what they say at school!"

On the way, Hattie bites her thumbnail down to the quick. She doesn't want to talk about Olaf, but she has to! Otherwise what will she tell her father this afternoon?

The trees in the schoolyard are light yellow now, but the maple up on the hill is flaming orange. On the gravel, signs of wild horse play can be seen, with branches all over the place for jumps. Hattie steps through the high wooden doors. "I have a donkey," she whispers. She can hear how idiotic it sounds.

The teacher is standing in the classroom with his big beard. He's putting numbers up on the board while all the children rush in and sit down. "Right," he says. "Can anyone tell me what a hundred and twenty plus ten is?

Ellen puts her hand up.

"Ellen."

"Do you know what I did in the weekend?"

"No."

"I was just at the showjumping with Crumb, and we came fourth."

All the girls catch their breath and say: "Oooh!"

"How about that," nods the teacher. "So, does anyone else know what a hundred and twenty plus ten is?"

Jon puts his hand up.

"Yes, Jon."

"My dad bought a new harvester on Saturday."

"Goodness me, that's interesting," says the teacher. "But right now, we're talking arithmetic. Does anyone know what a hundred and twenty… Yes, Richard?"

"We made meatloaf," says Richard.

The teacher tugs in desperation at his beard. "If anyone else has something important to say about their weekend, please do so now, before we continue!"

Then Hattie puts up a trembling hand.

"Yes?"

Hattie swallows. "Yes…" Everyone is waiting. In her head she sees her father's smiling face. But she can also hear the hysterical laughter of her classmates. "I have…someone new living next door."

"Is that so?" says the teacher.

"Yes!" says Hattie. "He's called Olaf."

Someone laughs. The teacher raises an eyebrow.

Hattie nods. "Mmm yes, but he is very argumentative. He bellows and kicks, and my parents don't know what to do!"

At once everyone is extremely interested in Hattie's story about the very strange Olaf. The teacher puts down his marker and listens as Hattie goes on.

"Olaf moved in on Friday. He's bought an old house by the sand quarry in the woods. And when my parents went to say hello, he just snorted and slammed the door. Then all night they heard him running wild and they hardly got a wink of sleep."

The class shudders. Imagine living next door to someone like that!

At break time, the children gather around Hattie. She gets to climb up on the coat room windowsill and sit there like a real storyteller.

And so the story of Olaf grows.

Well. Hattie has seen alcohol bottles in the ditch

outside Olaf's cottage. He has an Alsatian that barks when you go past, and no fewer than three white horses in the stable. Can you imagine! Three white horses that Hattie can come and ride every day!

Everyone's eyes grow big and round.

"They're show jumpers and they've won masses of prizes," says Hattie.

"Wow, lucky you," whispers Karin.

Ellen tugs at Hattie's sleeve. "You can come home with me to meet Crumb if I can come and meet Olaf," she says.

Hattie shrugs. "We'll see."

How easy it is to talk about Olaf. And how jealous everyone is. The part about the horses, that was pretty much the icing on the cake.

The girls charge outside. They run in circles and neigh. But now they aren't just any old horses, they're *white* horses. Shining white horses that prance with shining hooves. Hattie stands on the steps and watches them. You could almost say they're *her* horses.

Linda comes over. "Fancy you having that angry guy Olaf next door," she says.

Hattie nods. "Yeah, he's practically crazy."

"And yet you're allowed to go and ride his horses. Isn't that strange?"

Hattie's cheeks turn red. Actually, she could tell Linda the truth, but right now the story is working out so beautifully, she doesn't want to ruin it.

"Well, he's not as angry with children," she mumbles. Then she runs over to the girls.

She picks up a stick to use as a whip, because if they're her horses, they must obey her slightest wish!

"Lift your hooves!" she shrieks. "Lift!"

The girls lift their hooves high, higher. Karin knees herself in the face and starts to cry.

Hattie just laughs. "You're the clumsiest horse I've ever had," she says. "Trot!"

Every break time she gets to stand there and yell, and the girls have to lift their hooves higher and higher. By the end of the day, everyone's trousers are brown with dust. And Hattie still has the whip in her hand. Her voice is tired from all the shouting and her head is tired from all her stories.

When the school bus rolls onto Ängatorp's gravel road, many children crane their necks to see.

"Where does Olaf live?" they wonder.

Hattie quickly points to a narrow path running into the woods. It's the path to the quarry. "There," she says. "He's in there mostly."

Ellen waves when Hattie hops off. "See you tomorrow," she says. "Don't forget that I might be able to come home with you one day!"

Hattie walks with heavy steps through the garden. On top of the compost heap, like a scabby knock-kneed king, stands Olaf. He can't be seen from the road, so that's something. Hattie sighs deeply. She started to like her own Olaf while she was at school. She doesn't like this troublemaker at all.

Her father comes over with the oat bucket in his hand. His eyes twinkle. "How did it go? Did you tell everyone?"

Hattie nods. "Mmm."

"Were they envious?"

"Yes, a lot. They went crazy."

Papa is pleased. "You know what?" he says. "I think you'll be able to ride him one day."

Hattie tries to smile. "No, I don't need to."

"Yes, I promise you will."

He puts his hands to his mouth like a trumpet. "Hear that, Olaf? One day Hattie will ride you. So there!"

Olaf looks with his nasty eyes at Papa. Then he throws his head back. "Heeee-hawwww!" He squeals and squeals, kicks and kicks. Almost as if he's saying: No! No one can ever ride me. Never!

Hattie's father sighs. He puts the bucket of oats inside the fence and takes Hattie's hand. Leaves fall as they wander back through the garden. Soon it will be October.

Tony in Hackvad

October comes at great speed. Olaf stubbornly refuses to be nicer. Every night he stands in the field and bellows as if he's paid to.

Then November arrives. The cold creeps over Ängatorp's lawns and crunches underfoot in the mornings when they go out to give Olaf his oats. Across the paddock lies a thick fog that turns pink in the sunrise. Soon the fog lifts and then you can see far away over the frozen crop stubble. You can almost see all the way to Hackvad, but not quite.

But one night something can be seen in the dark, right where Hackvad should be. A flame of light shoots up to the sky. The family lie asleep in their beds, and the sheep are asleep in their stable. The only creature to see the fire is Olaf. His ears prick with curiosity because he's never seen fire before. A normal animal, such as a horse, would be terrified and try to run away from it. But Olaf isn't normal and he edges closer. Except he can't cross the stream. He stands there until the flames go out, and then he squeals a bit, just because. Then he trots off for a cranky little adventure in the bare woods.

The next day is pandemonium! The telephone rings at Ängatorp. Mama answers. It's Britt, Uncle Nisse's wife. She tells Mama that Tony set a garage on fire! Yes, Hattie's cousin. It was last night. Tony and his cousin Edwin were out driving around in Hackvad with the other moped-heads. Suddenly they came across an old garage on the edge of the village, so they took out their matchboxes and burnt the whole thing down. The police came with their sirens blaring and took Tony and the other moped-heads home. Now Tony has to work at the cemetery for the whole summer to pay the poor man who owned the garage. Britt is sad, so sad. What has she done to deserve such a boy for a son?

Mama says Tony probably didn't mean to be so stupid. He just wanted to test out the matches a bit, which is the sort of thing you do when you're fifteen. But Britt cries floods of tears. Now Tony has to stay in every night and watch TV until he turns eighteen. It's the only way he'll become nice again.

"Well…perhaps," says Mama.

Then Britt says that just this evening she and Nisse were going dancing at the town hall. So, she wonders, could Mama come and watch Tony for a while?

"Of course," says Mama.

She takes Hattie and they hop into the blue car. Hattie would rather not go but she has to. Papa has to work all evening and he needs peace and quiet.

Tony lives in a white house with a basement.

When they arrive, Britt and Nisse are already in their best clothes. Nisse has a shiny suit with creases in the trouser legs. It's hard to imagine that he used to fight with her mother.

Tony is nowhere to be seen. He's down in the basement, ashamed of himself, says Britt. Hattie imagines Tony locked up in a damp, cold cellar. Sitting with a chain round his neck and only a hungry mouse for company. That's what happens when you've done something stupid!

Britt takes Nisse by the hand and steps outside.
"See you at nine," she says. The door closes. At once
Mama sets off downstairs to say hello to Tony.
Hattie creeps after her with a cold heart.

There's music playing. Bad, screaming guitar music. The kind that was invented to hurt your ears.

Downstairs, Tony's sitting on a sofa, drumming his fingers on his knee. There's no chain around his neck. This is his room down here.

"Hi Tony!" calls Mama and hugs him. Tony gives her a quick, loose hug. "Hattie, come and say hello to Tony!"

Hattie slows down. She doesn't want to. Tony hates her. And she hates Tony. He has a denim vest and an ugly sparse beard on his chin. And she knows how hard he shakes hands.

Cautiously she puts out her hand. Tony takes it. First nicely. Then he gives it a hard squeeze. Hard enough to squeeze blood from her hand! Her fingers crack and crush together. Hattie howls and shrieks.

Then Tony grins and shows all his yellow teeth.

"Let's all be kind," says Mama, "and I'll make chocolate balls for everyone."

Hattie hurries after her up the stairs. If only Tony didn't exist. If only car racing didn't exist.

In Britt and Nisse's kitchen they take out butter, cocoa, oats and sugar. Hattie helps measure, which is fun when you know you're making something that'll taste good.

There's a black and white photo on the wall above the kitchen table. It's of a little girl with a ribbon in her hair and three boys with slicked down hair.

It's Mama, Nisse, Janne and Olle.

"Wasn't it awful having three stupid brothers?" asks Hattie.

Mama looks up at the photo and smiles. "No, it was wonderful."

"But they hit you every day!"

"Yes, but not so hard, really. And in other ways it was good to have them. At school, no one dared lift a finger against me because the brothers would be right there to tell them off. If anyone was going to thump their sister it would be them, they said."

Mama laughs and goes on stirring the mixture. Hattie doesn't understand the difference between one kind of hitting and another, but her mother seems sure about it.

Then the music stops downstairs. Tony comes up and sits where he can stare at the mixture. The fun disappears a bit. Mama tries to ask Tony if it wasn't a bit stupid setting fire to the garage. Tony says nothing, just mutters. Then he stops staring at the mixture and stares at Mama's handbag instead. It's open on the bench. A packet of cigarettes looms there in the dark.

When the chocolate balls are all rolled, they set the table in front of the TV. It feels almost like a party!

But when they return to the kitchen—Tony isn't there.

"Where are you?" calls Mama.

No answer.

Mama runs down to the basement to look...but is soon back. Tony isn't there. She runs into every room, calling, "Tony!"

He doesn't appear. Then Mama hurries to the hallway. The black clogs Tony always wears are gone! He's run away!

"Oh no, no, no," says Mama. "What if Tony's gone off to burn down another garage!" Quickly she puts on her shoes and rushes out. Mama's voice disappears in the darkness. Hattie will have to sit and wait on the cold steps.

"Tooonyyy!"

Then it falls deadly quiet. The houses around them are dark. Everyone has gone to the dance. A car rumbles somewhere on the outskirts of the village and, far away at Ängatorp, Olaf starts braying at the moon. But Hattie can't hear him. It's a shame in a way. She might almost wish that noisy Olaf was with her now. The darkness feels more and more dangerous, and Olaf is almost as good as a guard dog.

Suddenly she hears a peculiar sound. A moan. "Mmmm."

Hattie turns ice-cold. What kind of weirdo is out there moaning in practically the middle of the night? She looks around for her mother.

"Mmmmm!" Now it's even louder, quite close by. It's coming from Nisse and Britt's toolshed!

"Mama!" cries Hattie.

"Mmmm. Help!" comes from the shed.

Hattie knows that cracked voice. She stands up on stiff, frozen legs and tiptoes down the steps. She peeps in the shed door.

Tony's lying on the floor, white-faced and dribbling from the corner of his mouth. "I'm dying," he mumbles.

Hattie runs to the road and shouts at the top of her voice: "Mama, Mama! I've found Tony and he's dying!"

She has to stand and shriek for a whole minute

before her mother comes back. She rushes past Hattie into the shed.

Tony's still there, still drooling from his mouth. "Help!" he mumbles. "I think I'm dying."

But Mama doesn't think so. She twitches her nose and then she sees several cigarette butts on the floor. "Have you been smoking?!" she cries. Tony must have pinched cigarettes from her handbag when no one was watching.

With an iron grip, she helps Tony back into the house. Tony can hardly stand up; he hangs like a scarecrow off Mama's shoulder. Hattie has to carry his shoes because they fell off on the way up the steps.

Then Tony has to lie on the sofa, moaning and throwing up into a bucket, for the rest of the evening. Mama sits beside him and tells him off. "You must try to behave better! Otherwise you'll have to stay home with Britt and Nisse every night till you turn eighteen, and that's not much fun."

Tony says nothing; he just vomits again into the bucket. He can't eat any chocolate balls even if he wants to.

But after a while he can drink a little water, and then he tugs Mama's arm and says, "Don't tell my parents I was smoking."

Mama's eyes harden. "We'll see."

"Yes, we'll see," says Hattie.

At last Britt and Nisse come in through the front door. "What's happened?" cries Britt when she sees Tony looking all pale on the sofa.

Tony blinks at Mama. Mama looks at him long and hard, and then she says, "I think he has a stomach upset. Hopefully it's not contagious."

Tony smiles feebly. But Hattie is so angry that she stomps out into the hallway. She wants to tell on sneak-smoker Tony! What's the point of being nice to someone like that, someone who squeezes your hand so hard the bones crack?

Mama lingers at the door. "Think about what I said," she tells Tony. "If you feel like it, you can come and see us at Ängatorp. Goodbye."

Then she and Hattie make their way to the blue car.

"Why didn't you say he'd been smoking?" hisses Hattie.

Mama bites her bottom lip. "It's not good for

Tony to stay at home," she says. "When you're growing up you have to get together with friends and do stupid things. It's just part of it."

Hattie sits angry and silent as they head for home. Hackvad is asleep, tired from all the dancing. No racers are awake. No moped-heads are out on the prowl. Everything is calm and still.

But when they reach home, bellowing starts up in the field, as usual. "Iiiiii-hawwww! Iiiiii-hawww!" It's Olaf. He probably wonders where they've been, out this late.

Once Mama and Hattie have disappeared into the cottage, Olaf goes down to stand at the edge of the stream. He's waiting to see one of those blazing flares of light again, because it was somehow exciting. He has no idea that Tony with his matchbox is lying at home on a sofa being sick into a bucket.

Casper, Jasper and Moonshine

In fact, Olaf stands many nights down by the stream longing for a fire. But no one knows that. Hardly anyone even knows he exists. The story about the man next door with the white horses grows bigger with every passing day. Hattie has turned into a big fat liar. She can hardly open her mouth anymore without a new concoction slipping out about Casper, Jasper and Moonshine.

Those are the horses' names and she thought them up herself. And now no one cares anymore about Ellen and Crumb. Hattie is the happiest kid in the whole class.

She glides around the school like a queen, and all the girls follow her. "Pleeeease, can I come home with you one day?" Ellen asks.

"And meeee, me too?" says Karin.

Hattie shrugs. "Don't know, maybe."

Linda comes last, kicking at the frozen gravel. She's getting really tired of those horses.

One day in November the class is doing drawing. Hattie struggles with a horse; somehow it's not turning out well. The ears stick out and are too long. The eyes are narrow slits and the legs are all gnarled. She rubs it out and draws and rubs it out again. It shouldn't be so hard!

The teacher has his feet up on the desk. Wind blows through the bleak trees outside the window. Sometimes a few raindrops clatter at the pane.

A little note suddenly lands on Hattie's desk. She turns around.

"It's from me," whispers Ellen.

Hattie pushes her drawing aside and unfolds the note. *I have something to show you at break time,* it says. She turns around again. "What is it?" she asks.

But Ellen shakes her head and widens her eyes at the teacher's desk. "Wait and see."

The teacher hums and drums his fingers on his

knee. He likes art. All he has to do is sit in his chair and sigh happily at the heavy sky.

He's especially glad not to have to run out into the dismal weather at break time. The children can put on their raincoats and waterproof gloves, which are not at all waterproof, since they get soaked in five minutes. There are ice cold puddles in the yard and rowan trees that dangle their shrunken berries.

"What did you want to show me?" Hattie asks, pulling her hat down over her ears. There's nothing cold loves to nip at more than sticky-out ears.

Ellen looks all around. "We'll go to the shed," she says. "In case a teacher comes."

They go around the corner. Karin and the other girls keep up and Linda follows, not in a hurry.

In the shed the sand is still dry on the ground. Ellen puts her hand in her pocket. "No one's going to tell anyone?" she whispers, looking at them all.

"No!" they all say, and stamp their feet.

Then Ellen holds up six brown, shiny things wrapped in plastic.

"Caramels!" says Karin. "You're not allowed those at school. Can I taste one?"

They're all nervous. Treats like that are absolutely forbidden in school, they know that.

Ellen looks hard at Hattie. "Do you want one?" she asks.

Hattie can already hear her stomach crying out. "Yes," she says. As soon as she has the caramel, she rips off the plastic. The caramel melts like butter on her tongue, but slower, and then it slides warm and soft down her throat.

"Was it good?" asks Ellen.

Hattie nods. Her mouth already feels sadly empty. Ellen has five caramels left.

"You can have one more if I can come to your place one day and meet Olaf." She holds up the delicious caramel in front of Hattie.

Hattie swallows. She can't. She can't take Ellen home.

"No." She shakes her head.

Ellen adds two more. "What about three, then?" she says. "Three caramels!"

Hattie doesn't know what to do. There's a war going on in her body. Her stomach is shouting: *Take them!* Her brain shrieks: *Stop! Think what you're doing!*

She looks hungrily at the caramels…and when she finally forces herself to say "no" her heart is almost breaking.

Ellen rolls her eyes. "Why not? Why can't anyone ever actually meet that Olaf?"

"Yeah!" says Karin. "We've been asking for ages!"

Hattie stiffens. All the girls are looking at her. Even Linda, leaning back against the shed wall, drills her blue eyes into Hattie.

"Because, because…he's got sick," she answers.

"Sick?" Ellen raises her eyebrows.

"Mm. The flu. He can't even get out of bed."

Ellen sighs and puts the caramels back in her pocket.

"Wait!" says Hattie. "If I can have them all …then you can come one day."

Ellen hesitates. "All of them? All five?"

Hattie nods. The caramels have made her crazy.

"I could keep *one,* at least?" asks Ellen.

"Then it won't happen," Hattie answers, and it's almost as if she wishes Ellen would keep the caramels.

But Ellen desperately hands over all five. Desperately, Hattie takes them.

"Okay," she says with a dry voice. "That's that, then."

She tears the plastic from a caramel and puts it in her mouth. And before she's swallowed it, she puts in another. She has to eat them all up at once so she can't see them anymore.

"Don't forget now," says Ellen. "You promised I can come and meet Olaf."

"Yeah, when he gets better," mumbles Hattie, looking at the ground.

"And Jasper and Casper and Moonshine!"

"Yeah, yeah," says Hattie. She steps out into the howling, biting wind. Linda follows. The last caramels burn in Hattie's hand. She hates them. "Want one?" she asks, holding them out.

Linda shrugs. "Thanks," she mutters so Hattie can hardly hear. She puts the caramel in her mouth but doesn't seem the least bit pleased.

That makes Hattie mad. She's just put her whole life at risk for those caramels, and Linda looks as if she's been given three piles of dung. And why can't Linda ever be interested in Casper and Jasper and Moonshine? Everyone else thinks Hattie's the best in the world because of those horses!

"Don't you want to come home with me one day and meet Olaf and the horses?" she asks, almost as a command.

Linda shrugs again. "Not really," she says.

Hattie frowns. Why is everything so difficult? Why did she say yes to those caramels?

"Well, you can't, anyway!" she hisses and runs

away. Muddy water sprays up like fountains around her boots.

Linda is left standing, with caramel around her mouth.

Lucia voting time

The next day when Hattie comes to school, the gate is empty. There's usually someone standing there every morning. A small figure with a turned-up nose and freckles. But there's no figure in sight.

Hattie splashes over to the pear tree where she and Linda usually sit and laugh, hidden in the leaves. The leaves are gone, the tree is as bare as a skeleton. Linda isn't there either.

Hattie sees her over by the icy sports field. She's standing with her arms on the fence, watching the boys kick a ball between them. The ball goes every which way. It's hard to kick it properly with winter boots.

Hattie runs over with her bag swinging on her back. "Hi," she says.

Linda doesn't look at her. She looks almost as if Hattie doesn't exist.

Hattie waits a second. Then two, then three. But Linda looks resolutely at the hill. Then Hattie turns, quick as a whip-crack, and runs away. If this is how it is, she'll never say hello again! Who needs a grump like that who only stands and stares at the

hill? If only she hadn't gone over to the sports field! She wishes it was Linda who'd come up to her and said hello, and that Hattie was the one who wouldn't answer. Then Linda would have stood there like an idiot instead!

Ellen and Karin are on the stairs. Ellen looks pleased to see Hattie arrive. "When do you think Olaf will be better?" she asks.

Hattie's stomach clenches. What should she say?

But there's hardly time to think about it before the school bell rings. "Class is starting," she says, throwing herself past them.

As the children drift into the classroom, the teacher stands there looking cheerful. He has placed large, white pieces of paper on his desk. "Do you know what's happening in three weeks?" he asks.

"Christmas!" shrieks Richard.

The teacher laughs. "No, it's Lucia. Shall we have a procession for St. Lucia Day for your parents?"

"*Yesss!*" cry the children.

"No!" call some of the boys. But everyone knows they really want to, they just have to be a bit stupid.

Now they understand what the white paper is for.

"All the boys can make their own cones, and the girls can make their own candle holders," says the teacher.

There's a rush. Hattie quickly nabs a piece of paper. When she meets Linda, it's as if they don't know each other.

They each sit in a corner of the classroom and don't look in the other's direction even once. Well, maybe Hattie glances at Linda once, but not on purpose. She looks away just as quickly.

The candle holders turn out quite well. Almost round, with a hole in the middle. One by one the boys finish their cones. They look quite stylish when the white tops are put on their heads.

"Okay," says the teacher. "Now it's break time."

Everyone jumps up, sending the cones and candle holders flying.

"*Wait!* After break time we'll vote for our Lucia," calls the teacher. "Think about who you'll vote for, so you know when you come back."

Hattie's body turns warm. Warm and cold in turn. Lucia, that would be something! She can see herself with a red ribbon around her middle. She can see herself walking at the front of the line, with all the parents applauding and Linda, who won't even say hello, standing there regretting it.

In the coat room everyone starts whispering. "Who are you going to vote for, who are you voting for?" echoes secretively around the walls.

Actually, you should vote for the person with the best singing voice, because the Lucia sings a solo. But no one cares about that. Everyone knows that you vote for the person with the longest hair.

Hattie has quite long hair, almost the longest. But no one has hair as long as Theresa's. She can tie hers in a rosette under her chin. Also, it's blonde.

Linda sits in the big window and doesn't whisper to anyone. "Linda, who are you going to vote for?" calls Richard.

Hattie cranes her neck to listen.

For a second Linda's blue eyes look at her. Then she lights up with a big smile. "I'll vote for the teacher, of course! He'd be sweet in a Lucia crown!"

"You can't vote for the teacher," says Ellen, and she squeezes over to Hattie. "I'll vote for you, Hattie. You'd be perfect."

"Me too," says Karin.

Hattie glows. Theresa stands in a corner with her long hair. Everyone pats her on the back as if she has already won, but she looks worried. She might be scared that someone else will win anyway.

When the bell rings Hattie feels as if there's a pot boiling in her belly. Soon smoke will be pouring from her ears. She has to be Lucia or there's no point in living!

It's quiet and the atmosphere feels strange as the teacher goes around the classroom with a bucket. Everyone has to write a name on a piece of paper. You can't vote for yourself, and you can't vote for the teacher either, because it has to be a girl. Hattie bites her pen. On a normal day of course she'd vote for Linda. But now nothing is normal, and Linda certainly won't vote for her either.

No one will notice if Hattie votes for herself.

She cups her hand around the paper. But just as she's about to write Hattie, she thinks of something. If she doesn't vote for Linda, Linda might not get a single vote.

Of course that would serve her right…

"Ready, Hattie?" asks the teacher, shaking the bucket in front of her nose. "You have to write a name."

Quickly she writes Linda's name. As long as Linda doesn't know that the vote came from Hattie. And she'll never tell!

When everyone has voted, the teacher goes up to the board. He reads out the first paper. "Theresa."

He writes Theresa's name and puts a stroke beside it. He reads the next paper. "Theresa."

Hattie starts to feel like a heavy, dead stone and the third paper also says Theresa.

But on the next paper it says Hattie! And when the teacher has read out a few more papers, Theresa has five strokes and Hattie has three. Now her heart starts beating again. She can still win.

Excitement is high in the classroom. Sometimes Theresa gets a vote, sometimes Hattie gets one. Sometimes someone else does.

Now there is just one paper left. And on the board, Theresa has seven strokes, Hattie six, Karin one, Ellen two, Linda one.

It might be a draw, and in that case it will be a

lottery. Her heart thumping, Hattie looks over at Theresa.

Theresa swallows and swallows, her bottom lip trembling.

The teacher takes out the last paper. He does everything extra slowly to torment them. He looks for an eternity at the paper…then he looks up and says: "Linda."

It's like a punch in the stomach. Hattie can't breathe. A lump forms in her throat and tears are on their way. She can't stop them.

The sniffing starts quietly. Soon there are squeaking tears. Everyone is quiet.

But it isn't Hattie crying; it's someone else. She looks around.

Theresa! She's gasping for breath and drops fall from her chin.

"What is it?" says the teacher.

"I don't want to," Theresa sobs.

Everyone stares at her. Don't want to?

"Why?" asks the teacher.

Theresa rubs her eyes. She's silent for a quite a while. "I just don't want to," she mumbles. She says

no more. But everyone understands that it's because of the solo.

The teacher tugs thoughtfully at his beard. After a moment he shrugs. "If you don't want to then you don't have to. In which case it will be Hattie. Congratulations!"

"*Congratulations, Hattie!*" everyone shouts.

Hattie crosses her arms and looks around with flushed cheeks. "Thank you," she says. She feels a rush of happiness. Her heart turns somersaults and the corners of her mouth point straight up. But suddenly someone is patting her on the back. Ellen.

"How cool, Hattie," she whispers.

"Mm," answers Hattie.

"Hattie, when do you think Olaf will be better?"

Her smile disappears. Hattie stares at her desk. "Probably any time now. I'll tell you as soon as it happens."

By the time it snows

Olaf next door doesn't get any better. He probably has the world's worst flu. By the time it snows, he's been in bed for several weeks, and Ellen just has to wait.

The snow lies shining white over the school's tile roof, and over the church roof and over the woods. Now it's suddenly quiet in Hardemo. The trees don't move; they stand still and freeze so hard that their branches ache. No grass sways in the ditches, there are no tractors in the fields. Winter is silent.

But if you sneak over and put your ear to Hattie's classroom window, you can hear plenty of chatter inside. It's from all the mothers and fathers and brothers and sisters who have come. It's Lucia Day!

The whole class is in the tech room, stamping

their feet. The girls carry candles with white candle holders. They aren't proper candles but the ones with batteries. The boys wear cones on their heads and clean socks. The teacher looks at all the children and his eyes shine.

"How fine you all look!" he says, swallowing hard.

Only Alfie has spoiled things and written *Scania* on his cone—for Scania trucks.

Hattie's legs are twitching and jumping. She wants to start the Lucia procession now, it's impossible to stand still! She checks that her Lucia crown is straight. It's wound around with lingon leaves.

"But Linda, what are you doing?" asks the teacher.

Linda is writing on her holder. It's the words of the song so she won't forget them. She hides the pen in her hand. "Nothing," she mumbles.

Hattie sees her small cheeks turn pink. It's a long time since she and Linda talked to each other. Sometimes it feels like a hole in her heart: Linda, who's been her best friend since she started school and might not be anymore. Hattie doesn't know, she doesn't dare to ask.

The teacher shakes his head at Linda's scribblings. Then he straightens his tie. "Are you all ready?"

"Yes," they all whisper.

The teacher disappears into the darkness. Then they have to wait again. Hattie peeps at Linda. The light shimmers on her blonde head, and she keeps looking at the candle holder with the words on it.

What if Hattie goes over now? And whispers something to make Linda start laughing. Then everything will be back to normal again!

But what if Linda doesn't laugh? What if she just turns her head, or if she laughs in the wrong way and says: *Do you really think I'll talk to you?*

No, she can't. And now the piano's plinking. They hurry out to the coat room to line up.

"Night falls with a heavy tread…" They glide into the classroom where pairs of eyes glitter in the candlelight. A camera flashes and they stand in front of the blackboard with their hearts hammering.

It's all so solemn you almost forget to breathe. "Light Over Sea and Shore," "Three Wise Men" and "Christmas, Christmas"—they remember all the words. Only boys sing the Saint Stephen song.

Then Hattie has to sing "Silent Night" alone. The piano begins. She takes a step forward.

"Siiii-lent night! Hooo-ly night! All is calm, all is briiiight!"

She doesn't go wrong even once. The teacher quivers with pride on the piano stool, and everyone's eyes are on her, on Hattie. It's like a dream! A long, warm and exciting dream.

Soon the long line glides out again.

In the coat room they stop and listen. At first it's quiet. Then it's even quieter. And then...

Thunderous applause! Everyone has to run back in and bow. They bow once, twice, three times, and now the teacher turns on the lights so they can see how red-eyed and happy their parents are. Hattie's mother and father are sitting in a corner. Next to them is Linda's mother who works for the suspenders factory and her father who's always out in the garage. And there is Alfie's father with a t-shirt that says *Scania*. That's where he works, and he looks happily at Alfie's cone which says the same thing. Could you wish for a nicer child?

When the applause stops, the teacher offers everyone gingerbread and coffee. There's plenty of noise. Everyone has a lot to say after such a lovely time.

Hattie takes her crown in her hand and hurries toward her mother and father. They're standing and talking to Linda's parents, and of course Linda is beside them. Hattie slows down. When she gets there she holds onto her father's arm without saying anything. She just stares. Linda stares back.

"Hi, little shrimp," her father says. "You did very well!"

"Yes, very well," says Linda's mother. "Such a beautiful Lucia!"

They don't know that Linda and Hattie aren't talking.

"Mm," Hattie mumbles and looks the other way. Here comes Ellen. With Karin beside her.

Hattie feels her heart trip up in her body.

"Shall we go now?" she says, tugging her father's hand.

But Papa can hardly hear her, he just talks and talks.

Now Ellen is here. She looks at Hattie's father.

"Leave!" Hattie hisses. "Can't you see he's talking?"

"Hattie said I can come and meet Olaf some time," says Ellen, poking Papa in the side. "Can I?"

Papa puffs his chest out. "Of course," he smiles.

"Does that mean he's better now?" Ellen wonders.

Then Papa's eyebrows go up. "That he's what? Do you mean have we tamed him?"

Ellen and Karin look at each other. "Tamed?" says Ellen.

"That's right," answers Papa. "If you were thinking of riding, you can't yet—he's still too naughty."

Ellen's cheeks turn red and Linda's blue eyes blink in wonder.

"You have to have a good hand for animals," Papa goes on. "Donkeys can be a bit tricky."

"Donkeys?" says Karin. "Is Olaf a donkey?"

Now it's Papa's turn to look surprised. "Of course." He looks at Hattie. "What have you said he is?"

It's quiet. Hattie sees only black in front of her eyes; she might be fainting. Yes, she wishes she could faint and end up in a coma for five years! Everyone's eyes are on her. But she can't say anything.

"So there are no white horses either at your place?" says Ellen. "No horses at all?"

Papa shrugs; he doesn't know what to say anymore. "No, not that I know of," he mumbles.

Karin and Ellen stand there, lost for words, staring at Hattie. After an eternity they turn and leave.

Hattie sees them go over to Theresa and whisper. She looks over at Hattie. Then they start to giggle.

Soon there's giggling all over the classroom, except where Hattie stands with her crown in her hand. Mama tilts her head. "Little thing, what have you come up with now?" she asks.

Papa scratches his head. And Hattie can't even look at Linda.

No, she can't stay here a moment longer! "Let's go home," she hisses, her voice thick and hot in her throat. She rushes to the coat room and out into the snow.

With a burning head, she flounders over to the parking lot. Snowflakes swirl, big as cotton balls, and land on her face. Tears run and snot too and sobs burst out and disappear in the snowstorm. The blue car is buried up to its wheels. The doors are locked. For a little while, she has to stand and scream into the wind, before Mama appears with all Hattie's clothes on her arm.

She unlocks the door and Hattie folds onto the back seat. She doesn't say anything, just cries.

"Well, well," says Mama. "It's not so bad. Everyone will've forgotten in a week, you'll see." But Papa, who comes and sits in the car after a little while, says nothing at all. He stares in silence through the window all the way home over the white hills.

The fight

The morning after Lucia, Hattie dreads opening her eyes. Her stomach is twisted in a knot. Ideally Hattie would stay home today. She'd never go back to school. But children aren't allowed to decide things like that. Slowly she climbs out of bed. She puts on her sweatpants, then her cardigan from yesterday. Black, ugly, hateful yesterday.

Down in the kitchen, her father is eating a sandwich. He looks at Hattie. Then he puts down his sandwich and opens his mouth.

But he doesn't say anything. Silence rings in your ears far worse than noise does. After a moment he goes on eating. He must be angry—angry that she's so ashamed of Olaf that she couldn't tell the truth.

She can't eat any breakfast; she sits on the sofa

until they hear the bus coming along the road. Then she puts on her winter boots. She doesn't care about outside clothes but takes her Mickey Mouse jacket which is too thin. Nothing matters today.

Ellen and Karin don't say their usual hello on the bus. They pretend Hattie doesn't exist. But she can hear them whispering, and she feels their eyes the whole time. They cut into the back of her neck like knives.

What if Hattie could go back in time? What if she could say to Ellen: *I'll bring caramels tomorrow, and we'll be quits!* And what if Ellen said: *Sure.*

Just then they pass the track to the sand quarry. "Where did that donkey actually live?" calls Karin.

Then they laugh, she and Ellen. No, Hattie can't go back. Her lying mouth has ruined everything.

The bus stops at the school gate and all the children rush out. Not Hattie; she walks slowly. When she reaches the schoolyard, all the girls have gathered into a group by the steps. Their heads are pressed close and their backs are turned to Hattie. In among them is a small, bright figure like white asparagus. Linda.

That's the worst thing. Yes, worst of all is that Hattie lied to Linda, as if Linda were just anyone.

"What are you staring at?" It's Ellen shouting.

Everyone stares at Hattie. "Nothing," she mumbles. She turns and veers around the group. A pair of feet follow right behind her. So she takes off and runs. She doesn't look back, just hurries as fast as she can, throws herself into the shed and closes the door.

Soon the footsteps are right outside. Is it Ellen? She presses her nose to a crack and peers out.

It's Linda. Her cheeks are red. Then her shoulders droop and she tramps off through the snow. Soon she's gone. Hattie stays where she is. She doesn't know what to say.

When the school bell finally rings, she flies out of the shed and into the classroom. She puts her head on her desk and her arms around her head. She doesn't want to hear or see anything or talk to anyone. She just wants all this to be over.

The children drift in with wet socks and runny noses. Some giggle as they walk past Hattie's desk, and Karin tries to bray like a donkey. It sounds more like she's dying of suffocation.

The teacher is up at the board, talking about the time when all of Sweden was under thick ice. There were no schools then and no classmates. No sad fathers or stupid donkeys. The ice age, that was a wonderful time.

At lunchtime, Hattie shuffles up to the teacher's desk. "I feel sick. Can I stay inside and rest?"

"It's better to eat something," the teacher says. "Go and see if it helps."

The woman in the kitchen has made sausage and cheese. In the murk at the bottom, boiled onions swim around like transparent worms. Everyone has to take at least two slices. When Hattie has her tray, she goes and sits at an empty table. It's like having a terrible cold shower, sitting on your own. But that's what happens when you lie.

Or? Now Linda has got up and is coming over! She sits down right across from Hattie! For a long time, she sits quietly, poking at the sausage. Then she pushes her teeth forward in a smile. "A donkey," she says. "We should get one. Except, if you count fathers, I already have one."

Then they laugh so hard they bounce in their

chairs. It feels like having a bellyful of warm soup! The others stare at them.

Linda goes on poking at her food.

"Well…" says Hattie. "The reason you couldn't come home and meet the man next door… It was just that he didn't exist."

Linda nods.

"By the way, I voted for you for Lucia," Hattie says. "I thought you'd be the best."

"No way," says Linda. She'd never dare to be Lucia. "There's no one else to vote for in this class. They sing about as well as an old sewing machine."

Hattie feels happiness tingling up from her toes. How on earth has she managed so long without Linda?

And now Linda wants to know all about Olaf. She's never been interested in horses, but donkeys are something else! Hattie has to tell the true story of Olaf from beginning to end. When Linda hears about the bucket of poop that broke over Persson's shoes, they laugh again.

Then suddenly Linda kicks Hattie's shin. Alfie is strolling over. Ellen and Karin follow with their eyes.

"Why have you got a donkey at home?" Alfie asks
with a grin. He's strong. His upper arms are as fat as
loaves and he wears a cap in the cafeteria, even
though you're not allowed.

"Why not?" mumbles Hattie.

"Only idiots have donkeys," says Alfie.

"Why haven't you got one then?" Linda asks. She
rolls her eyes.

Alfie's grin disappears. He narrows his eyes. "Stuff you," he says and goes back to his place.

He pulls his cap down low and glares at them for a long time.

When Hattie and Linda leave their trays, Alfie quickly gets up. So do Ellen, Karin and some others.

They follow Hattie and Linda like leeches. Alfie leads them, shouting, "Donkey, Donkey, Donkey!"

He means Hattie. She walks normally and pretends nothing is happening, but it's hard. The word sinks into her stomach and soon more of them are shouting, "Donkey, Donkey, Donkey!" Everyone hears. They all turn to look.

Inside Hattie tears are welling up. Her heart is pounding, her cheeks are hot. When Alfie makes a snowball and throws it at her back, it's as if something goes BANG in her head! She flies at Alfie, her fists burning like fire, and next thing she's punched him in the mouth.

Alfie goes quiet and just stares at her. His lip is bleeding. He raises his fists, but in no time Hattie hits him again. And again, and again! Alfie throws his arms about. He gets her in the head and the

face, but Hattie can't feel a thing; she just hits and hits and soon they're both lying on the ground.

When she hears crying, she can finally stop. Blood is rushing from Alfie's nose. The others look at her with eyes like dark holes, full of fright. Alfie gets to his feet.

"I'm telling the teacher on you!" he wails, running away. His cap lies on the ground, bloody and wet.

Ice grips the back of Hattie's neck. This is the worst thing she's ever done. She's never hit anyone before. But she couldn't stop herself. Why did he have to shout *donkey* like that? He has only himself to blame!

It's not long before the bell rings. Hattie sees a drop of blood on the steps, and in the coat room there's a long red trail running across the floor. But Alfie isn't there; he's gone to the school nurse. In the classroom the teacher is so angry he's shaking. He storms over to Hattie and grabs her arm. "What have you done!?" he shouts.

She sits hard and cold like a stone and listens to the lecture. You're not allowed to fight! You can't hit someone so hard that their nose bleeds! You must talk with your mouth and not your fists!

Hattie answers quietly, only "yes" and "no" and "yes." Her hands hurt and her knuckles are grazed.

No one mentions that you aren't allowed to run around and shout *donkey* at someone.

In the end the teacher says she has to go to the nurse and say sorry to Alfie, who's lying there with a white bandage on his nose, crying.

Hattie gets up slowly. The sorry word. That's the hardest word she knows.

But now it's extra hard! Why should she say sorry and not Alfie? She, who had to walk away like an idiot, while a whole gang ran after her, laughing.

No, never! She throws open the classroom door, pulls on her jacket and stomps off. The teacher calls out something from far away.

The snow on the ground is still white and beautiful. But Hattie treads long brown streaks of anger into it. She hates bullies! She hates teachers who don't care if they're fair or not!

She goes straight up to the grove of trees, and there she stays for the rest of the day in her thin jacket.

Sometimes she kicks a rock or a tree. Sometimes tears run. When the school bus comes, she rushes over to it like a shot. She doesn't talk to anyone. All the way home she sits with her face pressed to the window. It's stinging cold, but her forehead is on fire.

Up on the snowy compost heap, Olaf stands stubbornly. He won't go into the stable; he'd rather freeze.

"Why are you so stupid?" shrieks Hattie. "I hate you!"

Olaf is silent. He gives her a long look with his narrow eyes. Then he turns and walks away. A lump of ice dangles in the tuft of his tail.

Olaf is gone

In the evening, the cats sleep in front of the heater. They wake and stretch crossly when the telephone starts ringing. Mama hurries over to answer it. Hattie and Papa stay where they are, quiet as corpses. Only the TV goes on chattering about things that don't matter. Tonight it will snow, says the newsreader.

When Mama comes back, her face is white and her mouth is a line. She turns off the TV. Papa looks questioningly at her.

"That was the teacher," she says, looking at Hattie. "And do you know what he told me?"

Hattie goes on staring at the TV even though the screen is black. "Yes," she whispers.

Mama puts her hands on her hips. "Alfie had to go to hospital with that nose."

"Yes, but he was teasing me."

"You cannot hit people like that!"

Hattie doesn't answer.

"It doesn't help anything!"

Hattie's mouth is closed tight, as if her lips are sewn together.

"And you can't just run away either!" her mother continues. "When the teacher tells you to say sorry, you must do it. Promise me you'll never hit anyone like that again!"

Tears are running down Hattie's cheeks. She folds her arms hard.

"Darling," says Mama. Her voice is soft again. "What did he say, then?"

"He called me donkey."

It only takes three seconds. Then Papa gets up and rushes from the room. The door to his study slams shut.

He stays in there for a long time. Ten minutes, twenty, almost half an hour. Then the door opens again.

"Hattie, come here a minute."

She gets up slowly from the sofa and goes into the

study. Papa is sitting at his desk. He's biting his thumbnail and doesn't know what to say.

"So, you've been in a fight today?" he says at last. "I didn't expect that from you."

Hattie tenses. She can't cope with anymore scolding. If Papa says one more thing, she might just as well die.

But Papa strokes her cheek with his rough hand. A tear appears at the corner of his eye. "Sorry," he says.

How can he say something like that? Hattie thought he was angry because of all the lies and the hitting. That he was mad because she was ashamed of Olaf!

No, now Papa is telling her he's ashamed of himself. He's sorry that he imagined a donkey could be the same thing as a horse. All the lying Hattie did at school, it's his fault, he says. That's why he's been so quiet.

"I'm sorry, little shrimp," he says again and lifts her into his arms. His arms are big and warm. Hattie's hair gets stuck in the stubble on his chin. It's lovely sitting like that.

But when they've sat for a while, Papa suddenly

gets up. Now he thinks he'll go straight to Karl-Erik's to borrow that trailer again. Then he'll drive Olaf back to Persson because he never wants to see that pain-in-the-neck again!

He rushes down the squeaky stairs. Havana the cat follows him, and Hattie can hear him marching out into the winter evening with strong, determined steps.

Immediately something feels wrong. Hattie doesn't want to give Olaf back. She wants him here at Ängatorp, bellowing and causing trouble as usual. Imagine Olaf being sent back to live with nasty old Persson, and it being all Hattie's fault because she didn't want him!

Quickly she steps into her boots and runs out. It's dark outside now. December dark.

Papa is halfway to the car. He's stopped there, staring at the field.

"Don't take Olaf back!" Hattie shouts. She catches up and pulls at his arm.

Papa doesn't answer. He goes on staring into the field as if he can't believe what he's seeing.

And with a smack in the stomach, Hattie sees what's wrong.

Olaf has gone. The field is empty.

Yes, that ugly, long-eared thing has run away from Ängatorp. The gate is bent where he's stepped over it and run into the forest. And Hattie knows why. Because she told him, *I hate you*, of course.

How could she say that to Olaf, never liked by anyone!

Papa calls out: "Olaf!"

Hattie closes her eyes and thinks, Dear good God, make him come back. And if you do, I'll be the kindest owner in the world and give him a sugar cube every day.

But Olaf doesn't come. The only thing that comes is the snow—thick flakes that land without a sound. The disobedient little donkey tracks soon disappear under a white blanket. And when the tracks are gone, it's safe to say, Olaf is also gone.

Christmas break

Once upon a time there was a donkey. He lived alone and bored in an old, dilapidated stable. One evening as the donkey lay asleep, a woman came hurrying in with her skirts pulled up to her knees. She was as round as a barrel, and she had a man with her. And guess what the woman did! She threw herself down in the hay and starting shrieking so hard the donkey was petrified. After a while, a baby plopped out from between the woman's legs. Jesus had arrived.

Yes, well, that was thousands of years ago. And when Jesus grew up, he never rode anything but donkeys. It seems he'd taken a liking to these splendid animals.

Hattie thinks a lot about Jesus and all his fantastic

donkeys. Life is so easy for some people. If you're Jesus, having a donkey is no trouble; people clap their hands whatever you come up with. But if you're a rotten little Hattie, it's another story.

The teacher, sitting at his desk and talking about the birth of Jesus, doesn't notice when Ellen pokes a hard finger into Hattie's back. "Hey, how's the donkey?"

Karin giggles. Hattie doesn't answer.

"You!" whispers Ellen. "How's it going with the donkey?"

"Shut up!" answers Hattie. It's so unfair that Ellen and Karin are allowed to sit next to each other when Hattie and Linda aren't. The teacher thinks they'll talk too much.

Ellen giggles. "I'm only asking."

"What's going on down there?" booms the teacher, who has finally heard them. He puts down the book about Jesus.

"Hattie said shut up," says Karin.

"Yes, because you were pestering me!" snaps Hattie.

"Just be quiet now," sighs the teacher.

"I only wanted to ask Hattie something about Olaf," says Ellen. "I don't know anyone else who has a donkey."

Some kids laugh. The teacher tugs his beard thoughtfully. "Hmm, not now."

"Please?"

"I don't want to!" says Hattie. "Can you just stop it! I want to hear about Jesus!"

"Mmm," the teacher murmurs as he returns to the book. Hattie plants her elbows on the desk. The classroom is dark. A little way off there's an empty chair. Alfie's. He hasn't been to school since the fight. His nose is still swollen and his lip is as thick as the sole of a shoe. He has to stay home and drink blueberry soup through a straw. It's awful to think about it. But even worse to think about what will happen when Alfie is better and returns to school. Because Hattie can't actually fight. It was just what happened when anger flew into her fists.

"You! Hattie!" whispers Ellen.

"No!"

"That's it, be quiet now!" shouts the teacher. "Is that so hard to understand?"

"I want to change places," says Hattie. "They won't stop pestering me."

"She can sit next to me!" calls Linda, who is sitting beside Jon. He smells of farm.

"No," says the teacher. "We know how that goes. You two can't stay quiet for five minutes."

"Yes! I promise!" says Hattie. "Can't I move over to Linda? Jon can sit here beside Patrick."

The teacher narrows his eyes. Then he shakes his head. "No, this is what we'll do. Hattie, you and Linda swap places. That will keep you away from the girls, if they're finding it so hard to stop teasing you."

Hattie sighs. Slowly she and Linda gather up all their things. When they're done, Hattie sits beside Jon. The smell of farm sneaks into her nose.

The teacher goes on reading.

But after a moment Linda jumps. "Stop it!" she hisses at Ellen and Karin.

Ellen lifts her arms. "We did nothing!"

"Well who pinched my back then?" asks Linda.

The teacher thumps the book on the desk. "Can we not have even a moment's peace this last day of the term? What are you two up to?"

"Nothing!" cries Karin. "We did nothing!"

"Someone pinched me in the back!"

"Teacher, I don't want to sit beside Hattie!" squeaks Jon.

"And why not?"

"She smells of soap. My mother says the perfume in soap gives me asthma."

The teacher's face is as red as a Christmas cheese. He looks as if he could explode any moment.

"Yes, I'm not going to sit in front of these two," mutters Linda, glaring at Ellen and Karin. "As soon as you stop watching, they pinch you."

"No, we don't," Ellen snaps.

The teacher rubs his temples and closes his eyes. "Okay," he says. "This is what we'll do. Ellen will go and sit beside Jon."

"No!" squeaks Ellen.

"Karin will sit beside Patrick," continues the teacher. "And Hattie and Linda can take Karin and Ellen's places if they *promise* to be quiet and good when the spring term begins."

"Yes!" shriek Hattie and Linda. They leap up from their desks and gather all their things again.

Ellen and Karin begin to furiously pack theirs. For ages, the class sits and waits for the teacher to go on reading.

Finally, they're sitting next to each other, Hattie and Linda. There's a song in their bellies.

"So," says the teacher. "At last."

And while snowflakes fall outside the window, the teacher carries on with his long story of how Jesus came to be. The strangest thing is that the wise men knew where to find Jesus, just by following a star. They didn't get lost once!

"But of course, it was no ordinary star," he says. "It was the biggest and brightest of them all: the star of Bethlehem." And when the men arrived, they found Jesus, newborn and wrinkled in a manger. The angels sang and the shepherds played their flutes and everyone was so happy they burst into song.

Suddenly Linda jumps.

"What is it?" whispers Hattie.

Linda's eyes glitter. "Well, I just remembered who pinched me in the back."

"Really?"

"It was me!"

Hattie can't hold on. Her body will burst if she can't laugh. Linda has to too. The giggling grows, and soon everyone is looking at them.

And the teacher slowly lowers his book. He glares at them, dark as a thundercloud. "Wasn't it you two who promised just now to be quiet and good if you were allowed to sit together?" he asks.

Linda and Hattie just laugh and laugh. "Yes," replies Hattie. "But…"

"But what?"

"But we only promised to be quiet when the spring term starts!"

The teacher drops his head to the desk. "I give up," he says. "That's it for the year. The end. Happy Christmas."

"Happy Christmas!" they all shriek and jump up from their desks. In a few seconds, the classroom is empty. Only the teacher remains, enjoying the silence.

Now it's winter break at last. A long white break that smells of wet gloves, wood fires, fir and gum. A holiday without Ellen or Karin and without an empty, glaring desk that reminds Hattie that she broke someone's nose. Yes, it will be perfect.

But even though it feels pretty good to be sitting on the bus and heading for home, something's not quite right. The fact that there's no troublemaker standing and waiting on the compost heap when she arrives. It looks like it will be a break without Olaf either.

A star in the sky

Weeks without school and without Olaf, that's a bit strange. Empty, somehow, with the nights long and quiet. Hattie can't sleep; she's got more or less used to the sound of that cranky donkey braying in the night. She can't understand how she ever hated Olaf. Now he's gone, he's the only thing she cares about. If she were given fifty white horses instead, she wouldn't want them. She hides her face under the pillow, squeezes her eyes shut and tries not to think about her poor donkey walking around in the forest and bellowing. He's stuck in her head like glue and she can't forget him!

Except on New Year's Eve when she forgets him a little because Linda phones.

"If you're missing him so much, it's best I come

over," she says. "I can be almost as nice as a donkey." She raises her voice. "Dad! Can you drive me over to Hattie's?"

Half an hour later, a red car skids in to Ängatorp. Linda hops out and the car disappears as fast as it arrived. Linda steps in with a sports bag in her hand. She only wanted one thing for Christmas.

"Did you get the moped?" asks Hattie.

"No," says Linda.

"What did you get?"

Linda unzips the bag. Inside are two white boots with blades. "Skates. What did you get?"

Hattie smiles. "You'll see."

She rushes up the stairs and into her room. Her present is on the bed. The fabric kind of glows and the clips are shiny like silver.

"A shoulder bag!" says Linda.

"Mm."

It's a green bag with a band that you hang over your shoulder. When Hattie had opened the box on Christmas Eve, it was as if she'd wanted exactly that bag all her life. She hadn't known till then how tired she was of her silly old backpack.

"Really cool," says Linda. "I should have asked for one of those instead. I should have known they'd never buy me a moped."

Hattie hangs the bag on her shoulder and goes to the mirror. Yes, that's exactly what it should look like. Ha ha, now they'll be ashamed, all those people who called her a donkey! At least no one except her has a real shoulder bag!

Linda pokes carefully at her new skates. They're razor sharp, and if you cut yourself, it can go right to the bone. "Can you skate?" she asks.

Hattie nods energetically. Of course she can!

In the wardrobe are her own old skates, smelling like mildew.

"The pond in the field is frozen," Hattie says, putting her arms in her jacket. "We can go there."

"Is it hard?"

"No, not too bad," Hattie answers. She knows how easy it is because of those ice princesses on TV. If they can do it, so can Hattie and Linda!

They open the heavy outside door.

Just then Hattie's mother comes into the hallway. When she sees the skates in their arms she rushes to the wardrobe and rustles around. "You must have helmets if you're going skating," she says.

Hattie hates helmets. At least she hates the Ängatorp helmets; they aren't ice-hockey helmets. They're crash helmets. A crash helmet is so thick that even if you fell from the sky your head would be all right.

"Yuck," says Mama when she finds a little black rat poo in one of the crash helmets. The rat has been chewing on the chin strap, so it's frayed. Mama throws away the poo and puts the helmet on Hattie's head. "Those blinking animals chew at everything," she sighs. Then she puts the other helmet on Linda.

The cold bites their cheeks when they go outside, and the heavy helmets make their heads wobble. The big maple tree glistens with a thousand million crystals.

Up beside the pond, they sit on the ground and lace up their skates. Then they step out carefully onto the ice.

At once there's a *scritch!* and Hattie falls flat on her back, and a second later, *whoosh!* Linda is beside her.

They soon get up again. The skates dance and skitter as if they have a life of their own. *Bang,* and Hattie has fallen again. *Boom,* and Linda has too. It's certainly much harder to skate than Hattie remembers.

It's not long before they sit down on the edge and sigh. This hasn't turned out as they imagined.

"Actually, I wonder what sort of idiot came up with the idea of skating on ice," Linda mutters.

"What?" Hattie asks.

"Well, watch this!" Linda stands up. She runs off over the field and takes a flying leap. "It's not hard, as long as you stay on the hill!" Hattie tries too. Linda is right. The blades stick in the frozen ground like knives. You don't fall over!

Now the helmets fly off and Hattie and Linda begin to dance this way and that. They leap and fly, jump and turn, throw themselves into pirouettes and glide over the furrows. The ice princesses on TV would be green with envy!

The skates squeak in complaint, but no one hears them.

"I told you it wasn't hard!" calls Hattie.

"Yes!" says Linda. "Skating is the easiest thing I know!"

They skate until the sun sinks behind the tops of the fir trees and their shadows are as long as ladders. Then they sit down to unlace their skates.

Suddenly they realize something. The blades are no longer sharp. They're as blunt as slices of cheese. Linda bites her finger. "Uh-oh. Momma will be mad."

Hattie swallows. Her mother won't be pleased either. Skates are expensive.

So as they trudge home in the sunset, they decide it's best to say nothing about the blades. In the house, they put the snowy skates in the wardrobe and cover them with scarves. "Quick, before anyone comes," says Hattie, closing the door.

Just then, her mother appears. "Hello!" she says. "Did the skating go well?"

"Yes, not bad," says Hattie. Then she quickly runs away with Linda close behind.

In the kitchen, Papa is at the stove, and the cat Stick is under the table, gobbling down little pink shells.

"What's for dinner?" asks Hattie.

"Shrimp gratin," says Papa.

That's what you eat for New Year. Party food. Soon the table is set with napkins and wine glasses, and it's all so formal you might think you've come to a castle!

It's a going to be a wonderful evening. In the hall there's a box of fireworks that they'll let off at midnight. Linda and Hattie raise their glasses ten and twenty times with strawberry drink. Cheers to the New Year!

But suddenly Hattie gets a sharp pain in her stomach. The New Year, it's starting without Olaf! Hattie looks out through the window. The field is empty and the sky as black as coal. The stars are white, cold dots far, far away. The one that shines the brightest is the one the wise men followed once upon a time to find Jesus. The Bethlehem star...

Hattie stares for a long time at the dotted sky. And suddenly she has an idea. A brilliant, clear idea!

At ten to twelve, they begin to get ready. "Now we can go out and light the fireworks," says Papa.

They run out to the hall. Boots go on, and coats,

hats and gloves. But suddenly Mama gives a howl. "What's all this wet?!" she cries.

Everyone looks at the floor. There's a puddle. It's leaking from the wardrobe. Mama opens the door and starts pulling out wet scarves and sopping seat covers. Finally, out come two pairs of skates. The snow has melted. She frowns when she sees the ruined blades.

"How did this happen, if I may ask?"

Linda glances cautiously at Hattie.

"Well…" says Hattie. "It was probably the rats! You know how they always chew at everything."

Mama shakes her head. She doesn't believe for a moment about the rats. And Linda's skates were brand new! What will her mother say?

Linda's nose starts to quiver. Her eyes well up, and soon her bottom lip is trembling.

Then Papa says he'll get the grindstone from the shed in the morning, and he'll grind the skates so they're as good as new. But now they have to hurry because it's almost midnight.

They all rush out into the black night.

Papa puts the rockets into bottles, and Hattie and

Linda stand back. Soon he lights the fuse…

Whoosh-bang! Whoosh-bang! Whoosh-bang!

"Happy New Yeeear!" they all cry.

Then, just as Papa is about to light the biggest rocket of all, the one called the Red Dragon, Hattie runs over. She whispers something in Papa's ear.

Papa looks doubtful. He glances at Mama. But then he nods. "Okay," he says.

And he directs the rocket straight up into the air, not angled over the field as he did with the others.

And then the Red Dragon explodes over Ängatorp's rooftops, lighting up the whole sky; it shines and shines, never going out. And anyone ten miles away, or fifty or a hundred, can see the shining red star. And know which way they should go.

"Now you know, Olaf," whispers Hattie. "See you soon."

Payback

It will take a while for Olaf to turn up. It's possible he made it all the way to the Finnish border before he caught sight of the red star and turned back. Then you have to understand that he'll need a few days to walk home. And while Hattie waits, January gets longer and longer. One day the bus is waiting out on the road, tooting again. School has started.

Alfie is better now. His nose looks a bit crooked, and on his head there's a new cap with *Scania* on it. He got it from his father.

"Papa says I should pay you back," he says when he meets Hattie at the fence.

She tries to go past, but Alfie blocks her way.

"Stop it, I want to get past!" says Hattie. A lump is growing in her throat.

Alfie shakes his head. He smiles. But it's not a kind smile.

"Here you go," he says.

At the last second, Hattie ducks his punch. She swivels around and runs away.

Alfie smacks his fist into his palm. "The donkey needs a thrashing!"

Then he comes after her. He has scooter boots. The untied laces whip around his ankles. "Come here and I'll thrash you!" he shouts.

No, never! When Hattie hears him getting closer, terror grips her legs and makes them run even faster. Her breath rasps, her muscles burn. Snow and gravel fly up from the ground.

Some of the class are playing tag by the shed. When they see the chase, they hurry over. Richard and Alex, Jon and Patrick stand back by the school wall, watching. Ellen too.

"Shall we join in?" calls Karin.

Hattie doesn't answer. She's just waiting for the punch.

But the punch doesn't come. Alfie is getting tireder and tireder, lumbering along in his big boots. "Come…here…and…I'll…thrash…you,"he puffs.

"I won't!" cries Hattie. She waits until he's really close… Then she shoots away like an arrow.

When the bell rings, Alfie is so exhausted his feet are dragging. His hair is wet with sweat.

"Hattie's the fastest in the class!" calls Jon.

Ellen glares behind her cold, foggy glasses.

Yes, Hattie is quick, quick as a fly. She runs into the classroom and she could carry on running all day if she had to. All week, all term!

Linda soon shows up, her legs wet after the walk from home. The rest of the class dribbles in one by one.

But Alfie hangs back. The teacher has already got them to open their writing books when the door opens and he saunters in. Ellen is behind him.

"Hurry up, you two," says the teacher. "Where have you been?"

"I was in the toilet," says Ellen.

Alfie says nothing. He sits down at his desk and folds his arms.

But soon he gets the chance to tell about going to hospital with a broken nose, and then he's a little chattier.

He could hardly breathe, there was so much blood in his nostrils! The nurses had to dig and scrape to get the blood out and it hurt so badly Alfie yelled. Then he was allowed to go home. His nose turned blue, then green, then a little bit yellow and then back to normal. But it will never be straight again.

Hattie swallows. Imagine being crooked-nosed your whole life until you die. Not many people want to marry someone with a crooked nose. Not that she thinks anyone will want to marry Alfie, but it still feels terrible to have clonked someone like that. Every time Alfie looks in the mirror, he'll remember Hattie and her hard knuckles.

Soon the classroom is quiet. You can only hear the faint sound of rasping pencils and the clock on the wall. *Tick-tick-tick*. Every tick brings the break a little closer, and then Hattie knows what's waiting. But as long as she has legs, she won't get hit! She'll keep running till she goes crazy!

When the bell rings, Alfie is the first to disappear.

In the coat room, he's nowhere to be seen among all the children hunting for gloves so they can go outside.

Linda goes ahead of Hattie down the steps. "He's not here," she says.

Hattie follows cautiously. No, Alfie is nowhere to be seen. Not on the gravel, not on the hill, not in the carpark. Where can he have got to?

Ellen and Karin come thundering through the door with Richard and Alex close behind. "Are you going to play tag?" Ellen asks.

Hattie is so astonished that not a single word comes from her mouth. She turns around in case Ellen is talking to someone else, someone Hattie hasn't seen. But there's no one else there.

"Do you want to?" says Ellen. "It's so boring with only four."

Hattie swallows and swallows. "Aren't you angry?" she asks.

"No," says Ellen. "Do you want to or not?"

"Okay," Hattie answers.

They rush off to the shed. "Do you know where Alfie is?" calls Hattie.

Ellen turns around. "At the rink! He said he was going to play hockey!"

Then it's as if a butterfly floats up and drifts about in Hattie's belly. Her feet leap all by themselves. Maybe she doesn't have to run, after all? Maybe Alfie decided to forget all about it when he saw how fast she was.

Ellen is waiting by the shed with her arms crossed. "You thump the wall," she says. "Hattie, can you count?"

"Of course," says Hattie. She stands with her nose to the wall. "One, two…"

"No, count inside the shed," says Karin. "Then we know you aren't peeking."

"I don't peek," mumbles Hattie, but she opens the door to the rickety old shed anyway and steps inside.

It's dark in there. Only a dirty little window high up lets in a streak of light.

Bang! Someone has slammed the door shut.

"No, don't!" Hattie yells. "I can't see! Open the door!"

But no one opens it. Hattie tugs and yanks at the handle, but the door is stuck as if it's been nailed.

And now someone steps forward into the light from the window. It's a big person with clumsy boots and a cap pulled down low. Alfie.

Hattie backs away, but there's nowhere to go. She's trapped.

"Don't..." she says. She gets no further.

The hard fist punches into her stomach. It's as if her chest is about to explode; the air in her lungs won't move! Coughing and gasping, she kicks and kicks at the door, and when she can finally make a sound, it's like a siren going off over Hardemo. "*Aaaaaaaaaa!*" She kicks and kicks, and finally the door opens.

Ellen stares at Hattie with terror in her eyes. When Alfie steps out of the shed, Ellen doesn't talk to him but goes off the other way.

Now the teacher comes running with a blonde figure close behind. It's Linda, who ran to fetch him. The teacher only has his inside shoes on his feet. "Are you all right?" he calls.

Hattie can't say a thing, she just screams. Her nose is running, her head burning. To be tricked like that, you could die from it.

The teacher glares at the other children. "What happened here, if I may ask?" he roars.

Richard and Alex are silent. Karin too.

"It was a joke," mumbles Ellen. "But we hadn't decided that Alfie would fight."

"We had!" says Alfie. "You're lying!"

The teacher takes a hard grip on his arm. "What do you think is good about this? What?"

Alfie shrugs his shoulders. "Hattie should get payback."

"No, she should not!" hisses the teacher. "You're completely crazy if you think this is the way to sort things out!"

Then Alfie looks in the other direction. He looks far, far away at something on the horizon. His crooked nose shines red and ugly in the cold. His eyes are shiny. "Yeah," he says. "She should definitely get payback. Otherwise it's not fair."

The bag!

Hattie will pay, Alfie is sure of that. But it's not enough for Alfie to get payback one, two, three or even four times. He wants it every day. All through January and February, Hattie runs, followed by Alfie waving his fists.

Today the pear tree in the schoolyard has just started thawing. It's afternoon break and Alfie has taken his backpack out.

"Come here, Donkey!" He swings his backpack in the air like a club, trying to thump Hattie in the head with it. It's a dirty backpack with a supermarket logo. Nothing like Hattie's green shoulder bag. Many are jealous of that. The girls in year five and six have exactly the same bags.

"Never!" says Hattie. "You should be ashamed of

that ugly old bag! I've never seen a more horrible backpack!"

Alfie stops. "You'll get it for that," he mutters. He turns and disappears around the corner.

Hattie sighs. Soon she won't have anymore run in her. Soon her legs will fall off. Her stomach hurts, like a razorblade cutting into her. She sits on the damp bench beside the gravel patch. How do you get someone like Alfie to give up? The teacher has tried many times, but he can't. Everything runs off Alfie like water. What if he never stops?

The school bell breaks into her thoughts. Hattie hurries to the classroom and sits down.

"Okay," says the teacher. "Does everyone have a completed story in their writing book for today?"

"Yes!" the class yells. Hattie too. She has written a story called Monkey's Moon Journey. It's about a monkey who flies to the moon and crash lands. He has to stay on the moon until he dies because his spaceship can't be fixed. She was thinking quite a bit about Alfie when she wrote the story. It would be nice if he flew to the moon and stayed there. Once a month they could send up a box of stale biscuits, and at the bottom of the box would be a note. *Now you're sorry for what you've done!* it would say.

"I want to hear them," says the teacher, with his eyes lighting up.

"Can I go to the toilet?" asks Jon.

The teacher shakes his head. "You've just had a break. You should have gone when you had time."

"But I didn't need to go then!"

"You'll have to wait," says the teacher, "Now I want to hear what you've written. Everyone, take out your books."

Linda rummages around in her backpack and Hattie reaches for her green bag on the desk hook.

But the bag isn't there. The hook is empty.

Straightaway, she turns to look at Alfie. "My bag! What have you done with it?"

Alfie shrugs. "What do you mean? I haven't done anything."

The teacher's face hardens. "I am fed up with telling you off every day!" he says. "Do you think we don't know you've taken Hattie's bag?"

"Teacher, I have to go, I'm almost peeing!" squeaks Jon.

"No, I said! Alfie, get Hattie's bag!"

Alfie looks out the window. "There's no proof."

Hattie slams her fist onto the desk. "Say what you've done with it, stupid!"

"Shh-shh, no calling names, thank you," the teacher growls.

"But he has to give me my bag," Hattie hisses. Tears come even though she doesn't want them to.

"I'll never tell you where it is," says Alfie. "You have only yourself to blame."

"Teacher!" Jon squirms on his chair and drums his feet.

The teacher sighs unhappily. "Off you go then. But be back here in two minutes!"

Jon flies out of his seat and rushes from the classroom. He has to clutch his pants so he doesn't go too soon. Alfie watches him go with a glint in his eyes.

The teacher sits at his desk. "This is what we'll do: No one will start reading from their books until you've told us where the bag is hidden. Do you understand? We can sit here until the end of the day if we have to. And no one will so much as whisper!"

Alfie just shrugs again, as if it doesn't matter to him. "Cool," he says.

Thirty seconds pass.

A minute. Nobody says anything. The teacher's eyes are dark as coal. Linda bites a fingernail.

After one and a half minutes, the door opens.

It's Jon. "Teacher!"

"Shh!" says the teacher. "Go and sit in your place! We will be silent till Alfie produces the bag."

"But teacher!"

"Silence now, just for once!" cries the teacher. "*Do you not understand what I'm saying?*"

Jon's face turns chalk-white. His eyes well up and his bottom lip starts to tremble. He has a thick scar, like a worm, on his lip. He got it when he was little and fell off the kitchen bench.

He goes and sits down. Sometimes you can hear him sniffling. Sometimes you can hear Hattie sniffling.

Then you can hear something splashing.

The teacher lifts his head.

It's Jon, the splashing. His pee is puddling on the seat of the chair and running down to the shiny, green floor. Jon hides his face in his hands and snorts and sobs.

"What's going on?" says the teacher in confusion. "Why didn't you do that when you went to the toilet?"

Jon cries and cries. "I couldn't because it was blocked."

"Blocked?" says the teacher. "Blocked with what? Paper towels?"

Jon shakes his head.

"Come on, what is it then?" says the teacher.

Then Jon reaches and points at Hattie. "Her bag!"

When Mama
was fifteen

When Hattie gets home with the wet bag, Mama is in the kitchen.

"But what have you done with the bag?" she wonders. "It was practically new!"

Then Hattie lifts her face and yells so hard the ceiling lamp rattles. "Alfie…" she begins, but that's all she can manage. She tosses her bag on the floor and runs upstairs. Then she throws herself on the bed and buries her face in the pillow. The soft Snoopy toy looks at her with unmoving eyes. He probably wonders why Hattie lies here bawling so often these days, but he can't ask. Whoever made him didn't sew on a mouth.

A brmming sound soon mixes with the crying. A small, slow brmming. Hattie lifts her head and

listens. Someone's coming
up the road.

She has to sit a long time at
the window, watching, before
the brmming shows up.
Eventually, a moped appears.
It has brown mudguards. Sitting
on the saddle is an ugly figure wearing
black clogs and a quilted jacket. Tony.

Soon there's a knock on the door. Hattie doesn't
know if she wants to go down. Actually, she hates
Tony. But at least her tears have stopped from the
surprise, and now Mama is calling her from the
hallway below.

"Hattie! Guess who's here? Tony! Come and say hello."

With dragging feet, Hattie goes down to the kitchen. Mama is so happy she's glowing. She's put the coffee on and is warming buns in the oven. It's not often anyone comes to visit Ängatorp.

"Imagine you coming all the way here," she says. "It must be cold on that moped!"

"F…flippin cold," says Tony in his cracked voice. His helmet is on the table.

Hattie sits on a chair well away from Tony. She's not going to shake his hand. Tony looks at her but doesn't say anything.

"Well, well," chirps Mama. "And how are things at home, then? Is everything okay?"

Tony shrugs and clears his throat. "I don't like coffee," he says.

Mama runs to the fridge and takes out the bottle of strawberry drink, then she sets the table for three. Soon they're all sitting and biting into warm cinnamon buns. They taste good. Hattie's heavy head is lightened a little by the drink.

Mama tries to make small talk, but Tony doesn't

really say much. He just looks out through the window and sometimes sighs a bit. Eventually Mama wonders if there was a special reason for him to come.

Tony shrugs again. But after a while he tells her what's going on.

It's just that life in Hackvad has become so incredibly boring since Tony burned down that garage. Just like Mama said it would be! He's not allowed to take a single step outside the door anymore, because Britt and Nisse think he'll go off and do something stupid again. He's never allowed to go anywhere on his moped, and his cousin Edwin can't even come and visit more than once a week!

Then Tony says the only reason he's allowed to come to Ängatorp is that Britt can phone and check that he's really there. Mama looks at the telephone. At that moment it starts ringing.

"Hello?" she answers. "Yes, hi, hi. Yes, he's here. Of course. Yes, it's all good. Yes, straight home. Okay. Goodbye." She puts the phone down and sits back at the table. "Well, well," she sighs. "I thought that would be the case."

Tony gulps some drink. "Can't you talk to my mother?" he asks. "I'm dying over there."

Mama sucks a piece of bun from between her teeth. "I'm not sure if that would work. Britt can be pretty stubborn."

She frowns and thinks for a long moment. Then she pushes her coffee cup aside and looks at Tony.

"When I was fifteen," she says, "I was in that racing scene too."

Hattie nearly falls off her chair. Never! Never can she imagine that her sweet Mama was a crazy racer! With a denim jacket and a pimply nose! Did she go around burning down garages as well?

"Is that true, Mama?" she says.

Mama nods. "Absolutely. I had a moped called Rex."

Tony takes a bite of his bun and looks interested. "Was my dad into that too?" he asks.

"Of course. And it was a wonderful time! But our mother wasn't so keen on some of the things I got up to. Once when I came home, I'd cut my hair short and started to use snuff. That was the last straw. My mother locked up my moped and said I had to stay home and knit oven mitts till I turned eighteen. Can you think of anything worse?" says Mama, looking seriously at Tony.

Tony shakes his head, eyes wide.

"But do you know what I did then?" Mama asks.

"No," Tony and Hattie answer in unison.

"I got confirmed. That made my mother happy again. I was allowed to take the moped out of the garage. I promised to grow my hair again, and I could skip the oven mitts if I only used snuff when she couldn't see."

"What does getting confirmed mean?" asks Hattie.

Mama slurps her coffee. "It's a church thing you do when you turn fifteen. But first you have to go many times to a confirmation group with lots of other teenagers. You get to talk with the priest about all sorts of things. About how to behave when you're grown up and suchlike. And when the priest thinks you're ready, there's confirmation in the church. Many parents think it's one of the best things you can do."

Tony stares at Mama as if she was actually Jesus. "Get confirmed? You think it'll work?"

Mama leans her head this way and that. "It's worth a try at least."

They sit a long time at the kitchen table, and Mama puts more buns in the oven. Tony is chattier now. He jokes and laughs with his cracking voice. In the end he feels so good he turns to Hattie: "Why are your eyes so red? You look like a psycho."

Hattie doesn't answer.
Her eyes go shiny again.

Mama sighs. "There's a bit of trouble at school," she says.

"Really?" says Tony. "What sort of trouble?"

And even though Hattie doesn't want her to, Mama tells the whole long story about Olaf and the lies and the nose and Alfie and his fists. And how Hattie who used to be so chatty has become pale and quiet as a ghost.

"Every day there's something else. I don't know what to do anymore," says Mama, poking at her bun.

Tony stares at Hattie. "What a little punk," he says.

Hattie hides her face in her hands. "He put my bag in the toilet too."

Tony looks at the dripping bag that Mama has washed and draped on the radiator. He swallows his drink in a single gulp, thumps the glass on the table and stands up.

"Don't think anymore about it," he says. "It'll sort itself out. Now I have to go home."

And off he goes to the hallway and puts on his black clogs. Mama and Hattie stand in the porch and watch him do a wheelie with the moped before he toots and disappears down the road.

What did he mean, what he said about Alfie?" asks Hattie.

Mama shrugs. "You never know," she says. "You never know with a racer."

Death

You never know with a racer. And Hattie wonders if she'll ever know what Tony meant that time in the kitchen at Ängatorp. Weeks pass and Alfie isn't the slightest bit nicer in school.

On the last day in April there's record heat. In the ditch behind the sports field, small yellow suns on stalks peep up from the grass. Daisies. They stretch and yawn and think that today it's probably Saint Walpurgis Night, and so it is. Papa is back home making a May bonfire.

In the classroom the teacher opens the windows wide to let the spring in to his wintry children. Then they hear the cuckoo calling from a treetop. He has flown here all the way from Africa. *Cuck-oo!*

"Oh my," says the teacher, with a peculiar smile.

"That was the sound of the southern cuckoo."

"What's the southern cuckoo?" everyone shouts.

The teacher explains that once upon a time people believed the cuckoo could foretell the future. A cuckoo heard calling in the south was a southern cuckoo. One that called in the north was a northern cuckoo. The one in the east was the eastern cuckoo and the one in the west the western cuckoo.

"An eastern cuckoo is the consoling cuckoo; it gives comfort. The northern cuckoo is the mourning cuckoo and comes with sorrow. The western cuckoo is the best cuckoo—it's the best. But the southern cuckoo is the cuckoo of death, and it says that someone will die!"

They all stare at one another. The cuckoo of death! Is someone going to die now?

"*Ha ha!*" shouts Alfie. "I know who's going to die!"

"Who, who?" says everyone.

"Hattie's ugly donkey!"

The teacher's eyes turn dark. "Stop that stupid nonsense!" he roars. "The thing about cuckoos is only superstition."

But Hattie feels an icy shiver down her spine.

What if it isn't superstition, what if Alfie is right? Olaf has been out in the woods with only snow to eat all winter. Maybe right this second, he's lying with his bony chest to the ground, taking his final breath. He's probably thinking, *Hattie, why didn't you come and find me?*

When she gets home, Papa is in the field arranging his bonfire, the one that will burn tonight. You light the fire to welcome May.

"Hello, little shrimp!" he says. "How are things with you?"

"Is it true that if the southern cuckoo calls, someone's going to die?" asks Hattie.

Papa lights up. "Have you heard a cuckoo, so early?" he asks. "That's great! Whereabouts?"

"Oh, in school," she mutters, sloping off to the garden. Papa doesn't understand that there are things for kids to worry about. For grownups, nothing is dangerous enough to worry over.

In the clearing beneath the big maple tree there are many faded crosses in the earth. It's a cemetery. Hattie buried shrews and half-worms there when she was younger. Death used to be almost fun. She'd put the corpses in the wheelbarrow and walk solemnly three times around the house, then into the clearing to make a grave.

Now death is not fun. She hates death, and she hates the cuckoo! Why would it call from the south? Does it even know what it's doing?

Soon Papa has finished his bonfire. His face is sweaty. "Now I'm ready for a beer," he says as he goes past the clearing. "Are you coming in?"

Hattie shakes her head.

"Nope."

Papa disappears inside.

Hattie sets off to the field. Her ponytail swings behind her. Far away the forest is like a black stripe against the sky.

"*Olaf!*"

Her call rises into the sky. If he's alive, he'll hear it. Then he'll come.

"*Olaf, here we are! Come out!*"

She stands silent for a moment. She peers at the fir trees. He's not coming.

But out on the road, Alf from next door is coming, driving a backhoe. He's probably pleased that the frost has disappeared from the ground. Now he's keen to do some digging.

The backhoe is slow; it creeps along. Hattie stands on the verge to say hello. Alf comes closer and closer. The big bucket with its blunt teeth gnashes and drools. Closer, closer, closer…

He waves as he drives past. Hattie waves back. When the tractor disappears around the corner, she looks along the road. There's a grass snake, flat as a belt. Death has come.

Then she's so happy she has to yell. It wasn't Olaf who was going to die! She rushes over the lawn and into the house. "A squashed snake! A run-over snake!"

Papa frowns. "Nothing fun about that," he says.

But Hattie races out again and gets the wheelbarrow. It has green handles and a big red wheel that squeaks as it rolls over the tufts of grass.

The snake is already cold. The little jaw is paper-thin. She lifts the body carefully with a stick and lays it in the barrow. She makes three solemn circuits of the house, but she can't help doing the odd little skip. You're not supposed to at a funeral; you're supposed to cry into a little white handkerchief.

She gets the spade from the shed. Now, here comes Papa! He has whittled two sticks to make a cross. It's fresh and smells of wood. But in a month, it will probably be as faded as all the others.

It can't be a deep hole. The roots in the ground are tough and hard to get through. But the snake is so flat, it's deep enough.

When the hole is filled in and the cross is in the ground, Hattie crouches and lays a daisy there. The daisy stretches and yawns and starts to wilt.

At six o'clock Mama and Papa come out of the house with matches held high.

"Are you ready?" calls Papa.

"Yes!" cry Mama and Hattie.

Papa lights a match and…*whoosh!* Off it goes, and the pile is burning. The flames flare into the sky. Soon Hattie is so hot and red in the face, she has to back away from the heat. Her eyes smart and her nose runs. But in some ways it's fantastic.

"Winter stooooorms out of our mountains!" Papa sings.

"Snow driiiiifts melt down and die!" Mama croons.

And others apparently take an interest when there's a fire nearby. Now someone comes strutting from the forest edge. It looks like a horse, but only almost. The ears are long, the legs crooked and the tail ends in a tuft.

Olaf! His coat is matted and he's as ugly as before. He's as stupid as ever, too. Normal animals run and hide as soon as there's a fire, but Olaf trots all the way up and bellows at it. "Hee-haaaaw! Heeeee-hawwww!"

While Papa runs to fetch oats, Olaf waits quietly. Then he just eats and eats and eats and doesn't look up once from the bucket. His tail switches left and right.

Hattie laughs. No one hears, not even herself because the roar of the fire is so loud, and Papa can't stop singing. But she can feel it. She can feel in her belly that the laughter is there, and it feels as if spring might yet turn out all right.

It wasn't only to welcome May that they lit the bonfire. It was also to welcome Olaf home.

Olaf's bundle

It probably did Olaf good to be away for a couple of months. He doesn't bellow as much now, and the sheep finally dare to go up and sniff him. But if Hattie or Papa try to get close, he backs off and his ears flatten. He hasn't forgotten Persson yet. It takes time to learn to trust people when you've been kicked like that.

Where Olaf has been all winter is a real mystery. How did he manage? Why didn't he starve to death? Papa goes back and forth in the garden, scratching his head. "If only I knew…" he mutters. Sometimes he stops and stares at Olaf, as if he wants Olaf to say something. But Olaf just flicks his tail and keeps his mouth shut.

One Saturday the pigs trot out of the sty. The

lawn is starting to turn green. Buds are bursting in Ängatorp's hedges. The big maple tree, which shades all the crosses in the clearing, is singing with life.

Saturdays are lovely. There's no school. Hattie can walk the plank on the edge of the sandpit and think about things other than Alfie and his fists.

In the distance she can see small, sharp steel knots gleaming in the sun. Papa has put barbed wire around the whole field so Olaf won't run away again.

Olaf stands at the trough, drinking. He's finally starting to look pretty good. His ribs no longer stick out and his coat has become a little, just a little bit, shiny.

Suddenly Hattie remembers the sugar lumps! The ones she promised to give Olaf if he came back that time in December. You have to keep your promises.

She sets off for the house, gravel crunching under her bare feet. She grabs the box of sugar lumps and rushes out again.

"Olaf!"

The sheep lying in the shade of the aspens turn to

look. Olaf eyes Hattie suspiciously. He pouts a little and tries to ignore her.

Hattie digs out a couple of sugar cubes. "Come on. You'll like these!"

Olaf sniffs. He knows they smell good. He comes closer. He stretches his neck, then his muzzle is close to her hand. He twitches his lips. His teeth appear.

"Telephone!"

Mama's cry rings in the air. Olaf starts and backs away. The fur rises on his back, and soon he has run far off into the trees.

Hattie sighs. She puts the sugar cubes in her mouth and heads for the house. The sugar box is left on the grass.

"Is it for me?" she shouts.

Mama shakes her head no. "For Papa. It's Karl-Erik."

Hattie looks around for her father, then stops to listen when he picks up the phone. "Yes, hello there. Hi, hello. Yes? Really? Yes, of course! That would be lovely. Six o'clock. That's right. Goodbye."

He hangs up.

"What were you talking about?" Hattie asks.

Papa's eyes look bright and curious. "Karl-Erik is coming for dinner tonight…he has something to tell us. So we'd better come up with something good!"

All afternoon they slam pots around in the kitchen. They'll have all sorts of food. Herrings, meat and potatoes, chocolate cake with almonds, and coffee.

"I wonder…" Papa mumbles as he stirs the chocolate mix. "I wonder what he's going to tell us…"

At five o'clock he puts on his shoes. "I'm off to fetch Karl-Erik."

He toots as he disappears in the blue car. The sky has changed. Recently it was blue. Now it's as purple as blueberry ice cream. The blackbird sings and a crow croaks in the distance. But the cuckoo doesn't make a peep.

An hour later there's another toot. A pair of headlights creep along the road.

"They're here!" shouts Hattie.

Karl-Erik and Papa come up the steps with Ronja close by. Karl-Erik pats his hungry stomach and licks his lips. "Smells very good," he says, stepping into the big room.

The pickled herrings are already on their plates. Cold, slimy herrings with bones like tiny hairs. Karl-Erik enjoys them and smacks his lips. Papa watches him the whole time as if he's waiting for something. But Karl-Erik only eats.

Then the meat arrives. Karl-Erik moans a little and thinks the food they're offering is far too good. He has seconds and thirds and fourths, and when his stomach has turned into a round little ball, he leans back in his chair and groans. For a long time, he says nothing.

Papa clears his throat. "What was it you were going to tell us about Ol…"

"There, there," says Karl-Erik. "In a minute."

Now the cake arrives. Karl-Erik takes a big piece and dollops cream on top. The almonds crack in his mouth.

"Mmm," he says. "M-m-m-m!"

When he's finished the cake, he takes an extra dollop of cream on his finger. Then he sucks it off and looks secretively at Papa, Mama and Hattie.

"Well…" he says. "Wait for it."

And so begins the exciting story Karl-Erik heard

when he was at the farm shop this morning.

Well, the man who runs the shop, he's second cousin to a woman who lives in Kärr. And that woman was at the doctor one day with a sore back when she heard something unusual: the doctor's friend usually puts out a sheaf of wheat every winter for the small birds, but this winter there was something strange about the sheaf because as soon as he put it out, after only one night, it was all gone!

The same thing happened several times and the doctor's friend of course thought it must be a deer or a moose that came and ate everything. But then he noticed that the tracks were a little unusual. They weren't horse hooves because they were too small, but perhaps pony hooves?

For several nights he sat on the steps to get a glimpse of the thief, but it must have been a very shy pony. It could sense at once if there was a person nearby and it would stay away.

Then sometime in April he got tired of this and stopped putting out sheaves. And since then the tracks haven't appeared.

Karl-Erik takes a gulp of his beer, enjoying it.

The whole family sit quiet as ghosts. You could cut the air with a knife, it's so thick with wonderment. It makes you shiver!

"What do you think?" says Karl-Erik. "Could it be our own bit of trouble, do you think?"

"Yes!" says Hattie. "Yes, yes!"

Mama and Papa nod earnestly.

"Well," says Karl-Erik, smacking his lips. "I don't suppose we could finish up with some coffee?"

Papa runs straight to the kitchen to make it. "Milk or sugar?" he calls.

"Both," Karl-Erik replies.

It's a while before Papa returns. They hear him mutter and grunt, and when he finally appears in the doorway, he only has coffee and milk. "I can't find the sugar cubes," he says.

"Oops!"

Everyone looks at Hattie, who jumps up from her chair.

"Oops what?" says Mama.

"The sugar… I'll be right back."

She runs to the hall, steps into her shoes and swings open the door.

Outside it's cold. Ice cold. You might wonder if summer really is coming. The dandelions that were shining yellow have closed to buds. Dew lies white around the house.

She hurries to the field. Even from a distance she can see the white box in the grass. Olaf is there too. But what's he doing?

He stands with his head through the fence. It looks as if he's trying to reach the box.

"So it suits you now?"

But when she gets closer, Hattie stops laughing. Olaf looks strange. He's staring straight ahead. His muscles are tense and he's dripping with sweat.

"What's the matter?"

Olaf doesn't move an inch.

And now Hattie can see what's wrong. There's blood on his neck! The barbs of the barbed wire have cut into his flesh and he can't get free!

"Oh no!" She darts forward.

Olaf tries to kick with his back legs, but it hurts too much.

Hattie looks back at the house. "Wait, I'm going to get Papa."

But then Olaf moans. He looks at her with his small eyes. Maybe he thinks she'll leave and not come back.

"Shall I help you?" she whispers. "Do you want me to?"

Olaf is silent. His body trembles.

Hattie grabs one strand of the barbed wire. Olaf flinches and snot comes out of his muzzle. Hattie grabs the other strand.

Straightaway, she pulls one strand up and the other down! Olaf pulls himself free.

Hattie peers, trying to see if there's much blood. But Olaf jumps round and shakes his neck. The blood has soon dried.

Then she throws a sugar cube into the field. "Here!"

Olaf doesn't even look at the sugar. Instead, he stands for a while and looks at Hattie. Then he trots away to the sheep under the aspens and lies down to sleep.

Taking the box, Hattie goes back to the house. Tomorrow Papa had better take down the barbed wire. Now Karl-Erik can have his coffee.

The donkey
and the poophead

Now you can see blossoms budding in the apple tree in the schoolyard. And in the pear tree. High up in a fork on the tallest pear tree, Hattie and Linda sit almost all the time. The good thing about the fork is that there's no room for a third person, so they don't have Alfie up there. But sometimes Alfie goes by under the tree and shouts, "Hey, Donkey!"

Hattie pretends it has nothing to do with her. But it does. Her heart soaks up every word. And the worst thing is that she can't shout anything back. If she did, Alfie would go crazy. No, it's better to keep quiet and just laugh a little. The trouble is, though, that Hattie's mouth is the sort that can't stay quiet for too long. One day when Alfie goes past and shouts, "Hey, Donkey!" it can't help itself. Her blood goes hot, her mouth opens up and shouts back, "Hey, Poophead!"

Some kids sitting on the benches by the lilac bushes laugh.

"She said Poophead," someone whispers. Linda laughs so hard she has to hang on in case she falls. But Alfie doesn't laugh. They can see his face with the crooked nose through the spring-green leaves. His eyes narrow. "What did you say?" he asks.

Hattie swallows. "Nothing."

Alfie is already climbing the tree. "You did!"

"No, stop it!" Hattie climbs further up. She puts one foot down and tries to kick him away, but Alfie grabs her foot.

"Ow, let go!" Hattie shouts. "I can't hold on!"

Alfie grips her foot harder, then he gets hold of her whole leg and pulls and tugs.

"I'll fall!" Hattie shouts and feels tears coming. "It's too high! Let goooo!" That's it, she thinks. I'll crash to the ground, break my back and be a little wet smear.

The teacher is sitting inside having morning tea and hears none of the noise. Linda grabs Hattie by the arm, but she's too weak and won't be able to hold Hattie when she falls.

Now some others under the tree shout at Alfie.

"Stop it!" yells Ellen. "It's dangerous!"

"Yes, you could break your neck!" shouts Richard.

But Alfie pulls even harder. Hattie's trousers end up at half mast, her underwear shows and tears burn her cheeks. "Stooooop it!"

Then a slow, distant brmming is heard. At first no one notices. But when the brmming gets closer and a moped rolls right into the schoolyard, everyone looks over in surprise. Alfie too. The moped burns seven, eight laps around the gravel, while the children stare. Who dares to behave like that? Who dares to drive straight in through the gate and drive round and round, making the gravel fly? And who has that sort of denim vest with rivets?

It's Tony, of course. Hattie's cousin with the black clogs. He steps off his moped, takes off his helmet and looks around. He has product in his hair and almost fully grown sideburns on his cheeks. At least if you look closely.

When Tony sees Hattie in the tree with her

trousers half down, he understands who is hanging
underneath her.

He strides forward. Everyone holds their breath.

Tony spits a gob on the ground and looks at Alfie.

"You look like a tough guy," he says.

Alfie goes red in the face.

"I wonder if you're the one I've been hearing

about," says Tony. "The toughest in all of Hardemo. Shall we shake hands? My name's Tony."

Alfie lets go of Hattie and jumps down. He puts out his hand. "Alfie."

Tony nods. He shakes Alfie's hand. First nice and loosely, as you should. Then he grips tightly and squeezes! He squeezes and squeezes, crushing Alfie's fingers into a bunch. They crack and Alfie howls, but Tony goes on squeezing. Then he pulls Alfie with him to the maple tree on the hill. The children watch Alfie standing, terrified and crying, while Tony talks.

When they return, Alfie goes over to the pear tree. "You can come down, Hattie," he says. He glances at Tony, whose arms are crossed. "I promise I'll never fight you again. Or tease you either. You've had payback for my nose now."

Hattie and Linda climb down to the ground. Hattie pulls her trousers up.

"Okay," she says. Then she runs over to Tony.

"Hi, Tony! Did you come all the way on the moped?"

Tony nods. "Yes. I'm sorry it took a while. It was

hard to get time off school. I had to tell them I was going to the dentist."

Hattie says nothing for a moment. It really is a surprise that Tony came here just for her.

"I didn't think you liked me," she says.

Tony raises an eyebrow. "Why not?"

"Well, because you're always mean to me. And you shake hands so hard."

Tony waggles his head. "Well, maybe a little bit mean. But I'm the only one who's allowed to be. If someone else tries to be mean to my little cousin, then they'll hear from me!"

Hattie nods. Somehow, she can accept that.

She glances at Alfie, who's standing with the others by the lilac hedge.

"What did you say to him?" she asks.

Tony smiles so you can see all his yellow teeth.

"Not telling. It's a secret."

"Did you say you'd kill him?"

Tony laughs. "I'm not telling," he says. "Well, maybe one day, but not now."

Then he nods over at the bright little figure with the sticky-up hair. The figure is staring at the moped with round eyes. Sometimes she blinks and bites her thumbnail, while her freckled face shines in delight. Linda.

"Is that your friend?" asks Tony.

Hattie nods her head. "My best friend."

Tony laughs again and calls out to Linda. "You! Do you want to have a turn?"

Linda swallows. "Yes," she says. "Can I?"

Tony nods. "Hop up." He helps Linda onto the moped saddle and then he sits in front. "But you have to hang on tight."

Linda waves to Hattie before she grabs Tony around his middle. The moped does a standing start. Tony steers out of the schoolyard with a sure hand. They disappear behind the fence and take a turn around the cemetery wall. Soon they're out of sight.

The whole class stays put. Dead quiet. The boys' faces are pale with envy. Poophead Alfie looks at the ground. Hattie feels like a blown-up balloon. Tony, that's her cousin!

They hear a toot on the other side of the cemetery and the moped comes back again.

Linda hops off, blissful as an angel. Her cheeks are pink, and her mouth can't stop smiling.

"Was it fun?" asks Hattie.

Linda nods. She's speechless.

But now the school's tall front doors open and the teacher storms out. "What's going on! You're not allowed to ride in the schoolyard!"

"This is my cousin," says Hattie. "He's a racer!"

The teacher is lost for words. "Really?" he says. Then he nods at Tony. You don't muck around with a racer, he knows that much.

Tony pumps his fist in the air. "I've gotta go now. See you, Hattie!"

Hattie waves back. Just as Tony gives full throttle, she remembers to ask one last thing.

"Tony! Tony!"

Tony turns down the throttle.

"Are you getting confirmed?"

"In two weeks," says Tony. "My mother can't wait."

Then he skids out of Hardemo schoolyard, leaving a sharp pair of wheel tracks behind him.

"Oh, happy you, Hattie!" Ellen sighs. "What a cool cousin you have!"

"Yes!" says Karin.

Hattie and Linda stand for a long time at the fence, watching Tony ride away.

"Do you know what I've decided?" says Linda.

"Nope."

"I'm going to be a racer when I'm older. For real."

Hattie is quiet a moment then she nods. "Me too."

Yes, when Hattie and Linda are grown up, they'll be racers, just like Tony. Then they'll wear denim jackets and black wooden clogs, and the moped they'll share will be pink, with one green handle and one red. Linda and Hattie together. They swear on it.

Olaf isn't angry anymore

Summer comes striding. Soon summer holidays will knock at the school's tall wooden doors. Soon they'll put birch boughs on the steps, the children will dress in clean white clothes and the Hardemo church bells will ring for ten long weeks of freedom.

But first Hattie has to go to another church, the one in Hackvad, because the whole family have been invited to Tony's confirmation.

Now Tony will step into the world of adults.

When Mama parks the blue car next to the churchyard, the sun is scorching down from the very top of the sky. But inside the church it's cool. The walls are made of thick, cold stone. Nisse and Britt are sitting in a pew close to the front. Britt is biting her nails. What if Tony makes a fool of himself? What if he falls over and goes headfirst into the baptismal font or if he happens to say a bad word to the priest? That'd be the end of confirmation, Britt reckons.

Now the church doors close and someone sitting high up in a balcony starts to play the organ. The priest comes out of the sacristy and everyone getting confirmed files in. They're dressed in white smocks, almost like a Lucia procession.

But not really. No one has a cone on their head and there's no Lucia at the front with a red sash around her middle. Instead there's Tony, holding up a cross.

Britt gets excited and starts waving. Then Tony forgets himself and waves back, and the cross almost crashes to the floor. But Tony is quick and saves it in time. Britt's cheeks turn white. She puts her hand to her forehead and leans on Nisse's shoulder.

Now all the young people go and sit on chairs right up the front, and as usual the priest gets up and speaks. Hattie looks around while the words echo between the walls.

Along the walls there are angels made of wood.

Their hands have fallen off and they all look like something brought back from the dump. Their wooden faces are sad, rotten and worm-eaten.

Hattie understands that you could become a bit rotten and sulky if you had to stand there and listen to sermons all day. She already feels that they've been in the church too long. She had no idea it would take so long to be confirmed. But soon the priest has finished talking, and the young people have also spoken a little and then it's time for communion. That's when you eat a little biscuit and have a sip of wine with it, and all this should make you think of Jesus' last meal. The one he ate before he got put up on the cross.

The young people kneel and open their mouths. When everyone has had enough, the priest asks if anyone else wants any.

Britt and Nisse get up. Hattie is quick to follow. She likes biscuits and can't hear her mother at the back whispering, "Stop!"

The priest laughs when she puts out her hands. "So, here you are."

Hattie bites into the biscuit. It doesn't taste like

normal biscuits. It tastes like paper. Worse than paper. The little bit grows and goes mushy in her mouth. Finally, it slides down her throat like a worm.

But there's a big bit left. She looks at the priest. He smiles. He probably thinks these biscuits are the best ever.

"I'll save it for later," Hattie mumbles. She pops the biscuit in her pocket and runs back to Mama and Papa.

"It's just for people who've been confirmed," whispers her mother. "Then you can taste it if you want to."

Hattie swallows to get rid of the papery taste. She'll never be confirmed!

Now everyone stands up and sings, and the young people process out again. It's finally over!

When Tony goes past, Hattie pokes him in the side. "Hi, Tony," she whispers.

Tony smiles. "Is everything going okay with Alfie?"

"Yes," answers Hattie because Alfie hasn't said boo to her since Tony came to visit Hardemo.

Tony goes off along the aisle.

"What's that?" whispers Mama. "What did he mean by that?"

"Oh, nothing," says Hattie. "A secret."

To the wheezing tones of the organ, they step out the door. The sun feels warm on their faces. Outside, Britt and Nisse stand and admire Tony's new workplace.

Every day for eight weeks he has to get up at six o'clock and water the flowers on all the graves. That's so he can pay the poor man who had his garage burnt down.

Mama clears her throat. "Now he has to work so hard all day, maybe he can at least take his moped out in the evenings?" she says, looking at Britt.

Yes, Britt agrees. Now Tony has been confirmed as well, which means he can't act completely stupid.

"Yes," says Nisse, who was also crazy once upon a time. "If you have racer blood in your veins, you have to be able to do as you like just a little bit."

Mama winks at Hattie and the family heads off to the blue car. Hackvad's fields billow green as they drive home.

In the field at Ängatorp, Olaf stands silently at the wall. He pricks up his ears a little when the car arrives, probably wondering where they've been. "We've been to a confirmation!" Hattie holds out the biscuit from her pocket. The barbed wire is gone now and only the old fence is left.

Olaf waits. His muzzle wrinkles a little. He takes a couple of steps forward and waits a moment longer. He looks uncertainly at Hattie. Then he sticks out his teeth and snatches the biscuit. He backs away. Soon the biscuit is in his stomach.

"You liked it!" says Hattie. "You're the strangest creature I know, Olaf." Then she goes into the house.

On the calendar in the kitchen, she counts the days till the summer break.

There aren't many, just a week or so.

As she lies in bed ready to go to sleep, Hattie feels it will be a good summer. There's no special reason for that, just that summer is always good. Linda will probably come and sleep over a few times. Then *maybe* they'll take the bus to Hackvad and visit Tony. Then they can shower under the garden hose.

And bike over to the summer houses to pick wild strawberries. And bury dead mice in the clearing. And go fishing down in the stream. And eat fresh beets with butter.

Yes, as Hattie lies there thinking of everything she'll do with Linda this summer, her eyelids slowly droop and settle down.

Her head grows heavier, and suddenly she's asleep. Her breaths are small and calm. Somewhere up in the sky, three white horses are galloping, tails flying. They bound over the clouds and soon they're gone.

And out in the big aspen, a tiny beetle is hatching. He stretches out his legs and sticks his antennae in the air. It will be a good summer; he thinks so too.

Several hours later Hattie wakes.

The clock says it's only half past five, quite a while before the school bus comes. But something woke her. Somebody screeched in the field.

Quiet as a mouse, she pushes back the duvet. She shoves her legs into comfy pants and her arms into cardigan sleeves. Then she slowly sneaks out through the door. Snores come from Mama and Papa's bedroom.

In the living room, the black dog Tacka lies and wonders what's going on.

"Stay," says Hattie. "I'm just going to do one thing."

Tacka blinks her brown eyes. Then she lays her head on the floor and goes back to sleep.

The stairs creak on the way down. Hattie steps into her shoes and opens the door. The dew is thick on the ground and in the air. A white covering of fog dances over the farm and looks like smoke. Hattie crunches over the gravel and walks through the garden. The rooster is asleep, the hens are asleep, the pigs are asleep, the sheep are asleep. But Olaf isn't asleep. He's braying, "Heeee-hawww!"

It doesn't sound like it used to, so frightful and hollow. This is something else. He's standing at the gate, waiting.

"Hey," whispers Hattie, and when Olaf sees her, he stops braying. He swings his tail and snorts a little.

They look at each other a moment.

"Shall we go for a walk?" asks Hattie. She climbs onto the gate. Olaf stands still, cool as a cucumber.

Hattie grabs hold of the short, stubbly mane. She

wobbles a little on the gate and Olaf shifts to keep his balance.

Then Hattie swings one leg over Olaf's back. With a single, careful hop, she's sitting there. She pats him on the neck as if this is something she

always does. "Sorry," she says. "I'm sorry I said I hate you."

That word, it can still turn up sometimes. At least once a year. Olaf snorts.

He couldn't care less about sorry, now that they're going for a walk!

He lurches through the wet grass. Two sheep wake and stare as if they think they're in a strange dream. But it isn't a dream: Hattie is now riding Olaf.

Because when she woke and heard him, she knew what he was saying. He was squealing that he wasn't angry anymore.

And when the sun comes up, they turn and walk along the fence.

Olaf stumbles now and then. They go slowly. But that's how it always is in the beginning.

This edition first published in 2021 by Gecko Press
PO Box 9335, Wellington 6141, New Zealand
info@geckopress.com

English-language edition © Gecko Press Ltd 2021
Translation © Julia Marshall 2021
Hedvig och Max-Olov
Text © Frida Nilsson and Natur & Kultur, Stockholm 2006
Illustrations © Stina Wirsén and Natur & Kultur, Stockholm 2006
Published in agreement with Koja Agency

Distributed in the United States and Canada by Lerner Publishing Group,
lernerbooks.com
Distributed in the United Kingdom by Bounce Sales and Marketing,
bouncemarketing.co.uk
Distributed in Australia and New Zealand by Walker Books Australia,
walkerbooks.com.au

The cost of this translation was defrayed by a subsidy from the
Swedish Arts Council, gratefully acknowledged.

Edited by Penelope Todd
Cover design by Megan van Staden
Typesetting by Esther Chua
Printed in China by Everbest Printing Co. Ltd, an accredited ISO 14001 &
FSC-certified printer

ISBN hardback: 978-1-776573-17-2 (USA)
ISBN paperback: 978-1-776573-18-9
Ebook available

For more curiously good books, visit geckopress.com

Gecko Press is a New Zealand-based, small-by-choice, independent publisher of children's books in translation. We publish a curated list of books from the best writers and illustrators in the world.

Gecko Press books celebrate unsameness. They encourage us to be thoughtful and inquisitive, and offer different—sometimes challenging, often funny—ways of seeing the world. They are printed on high-quality, sustainably sourced paper with stitched bindings so they can be read and re-read.

If you enjoyed **Hattie and Olaf**, visit our website or your local bookstore to find more Gecko Press illustrated chapter books. You might like ...

Detective Gordon: The First Case by Ulf Nilsson and Gitte Spee, for detective stories set in a friendly forest, where Detective Gordon seeks justice for all and always makes time for delicious cakes.

The Runaways by Ulf Stark and Kitty Crowther— Ulf's grandfather hates being in hospital, so together they make a plan to break him out.

The Yark by Bertrand Santini and Laurent Gapaillard, for readers who enjoy fairy tales and aren't afraid of the crunch of bones in a monster's teeth...